FREEDOM'S LIGHT

By

Robert J. Saniscalchi

Another Rob and Tex Adventure

Freedom's Light

First edition

This book is dedicated to our Veterans and to those who presently serve in our Military today.

"Courage is fear holding on a minute longer.
General George S. Patton

Freedom's Light
Preface

Stretching all the way back through the seemingly endless millenniums of time, there has been one constant, as sure as the sun rises every day. That constant is the relentless struggle of good against evil, and it's as relevant today as it was so very long ago.

On one side, we have the free, peaceful, hardworking, loving people who stand in the light of the Earth. On the other side lurk the dark, evil ones, hiding in the shadows, waiting to kill anyone unlike them.

The evil ones can't begin to comprehend what it is to be peaceful, to be free. They are always waiting and watching, making plans to down the innocent, to terrorize and plunder until their appetite for blood is sated. Not until the year 2001 and the shocking reality that no one is truly safe from the darkness of this evil did America and the world begin to wake up.

The stark reality of the brutal kill-or-be-killed mentality struck home, and finally, the righteous of the world began to fight back. From the ashes, they gleaned a great lesson. They learned to seek out the evil ones and destroy them. They learned that even in the midst of a simmering, sinister doom, there is always, always hope.

The sooner all of society realizes that we must stand together, the better. There is hope! In our combined strength, we will fight terror with deadly determination and at last put an end to this evil threat…and when we do; the world will be a much better place for it.

Chapter 1

The Beginning

Deep in the mountains of Afghanistan, a group of radical extremists (later to be known as the Taliban) gathered around their tall, bearded leader for another important meeting to finalize the details of a plan to eventually bring the world to a shocking new realization of all that such a ragtag group of fanatical, determined, and well-trained evil terrorists could accomplish.

They had been up to their nasty games as far back as 1983, when the terrorists began with a horrific attack on American troops in Beirut, killing over 200 U.S. Marines. Another attack, this time on American soil took place in 1993, when a bomb was placed in the basement of the World Trade Center. When were we going to wake up? As time went by, terrorist groups kept spreading throughout the Middle East, growing stronger in the shadows of Saddam Hessian and *Desert Storm*. Innocent people continued to be murdered around the world.

An intricate network of radical Islamic terrorists, to be known as Al-Qaeda (translated as "the base") was being created. They were low tech and stayed under the radar, yet they continued to be a deadly organization, even more so because they used a minimum amount of cell phones or computers that could be traced and lead authorities to them. They were almost invisible. Like tiny spiders spinning their webs, the evil terrorist were spreading out and infiltrating, working toward their ultimate battle, when Jihad (Holy War) would begin against the so called "infidels" of the world.

Back in the USA, the intelligence community was just beginning to analyze some of the recent terrorist attacks. They took a look at the explosion in the basement of the World Trade Center, but for some reason, so many isolated attacks around the world were never fully realized by our president and his military commanders as a direct threat to our national security—at least not until it was too late.

History was doomed to repeat itself, and there was a high price to pay for negligence, naïveté, and tolerance. The purely evil intent of the terrorists was difficult to even imagine. Our opportunity to stop them had been missed, our chance at victory overlooked. The evil spiders were moving among us...

Chapter 2

Bond of Brothers

It was a cold, blustery day in late November, in the year that was the dawn of the new millennium. The Marrinos were heading north on the Jersey Parkway, toward upstate New York. The driver of the SUV was Paul, locked in deep conversation with his two brothers, Rob and Roy. The topic of the day was deer hunting. In fact, the lure of venison and the thrill of the hunt were the very reasons for their annual trip to the family's mountain hideaway.

Paul, the elder among them, managed computer systems for a large accounting firm. Roy, a journeyman tradesman, worked in the Carpenters Union. Both were avid bow and gun hunters. The youngest, Rob, was 28, an enlisted man, working for Uncle Sam. He'd always been a sportsman, and he enjoyed hunting with his brothers, not so much for the kill as for soaking in the beauty of the great outdoors. Recently, Rob had purchased a new 50-caliber inline muzzle-loading rifle, and he'd fine-tuned it to shoot inside a 1-inch circle at 100 yards. He liked that it gave him a single shot, a chance. To him, it was a little more sporting than a modern rifle.

Both Paul and Roy were married men, settled down, Rob's military career kept him at a distance; thus, he always looked forward to this time of year. He'd invested almost a decade in the U.S. Army. A veteran of *Desert Storm*, he had worked his way up the ranks to become part of a Special Operations Delta Force team. It took Rob several months of intensive training to qualify and become part of that elite force, which was tasked with taking care of threats to national security. While he hadn't walked down the aisle yet, Rob loved his girlfriend, Ashley, who easily accepted his long stays away. Both understood and dealt with one another's independence, and that made her the perfect soulmate for a military man.

The military took Rob on intense, dangerous assignments all over the world, but every November, as often as he could, he eagerly looked forward to being home for the holidays, with a month of downtime. After all he'd dealt with in the last year; the good Lord knew he'd been looking forward to being with Ashley and his family.

The SUV was packed up with all the goodies they'd need, as well as plenty of beer. Rob remembered to bring his usual bottle of special brandy. The well-stocked vehicle slowly climbed the mountain road, and Rob sighed in delight as he peered out at the beautiful groves of pine trees, mingled with white birch and hardwood that covered the mountainside.

Roy slowly rolled down his window to take in some of the cold, crisp, clean mountain air. "Mmm," he said, inhaling deeply. "Hey, guys, you smell those pines?"

"Yeah Roy, Man, I love it up here," Paul replied, "but close the damn window before we all freeze to death."

"Okay, okay," Roy added. "I don't want you poor little fellas to catch a cold or anything. You're gonna be feelin' poor enough when I bag the big buck tomorrow."

"Yeah, right," Rob retorted with a snort and an eye-roll. "You forgot I've got my new rifle. I could shoot that buck from 200 yards out, no problem!"

Paul smiled as he lit up another smoke. "We'll soon see who gets what, my friends. I just hope you guys can walk the walk as good as you talk the talk, or Bambi's gonna be laughin' at you just as hard as I am."

The brotherly banter and laughter continued as the SUV climbed higher and higher up the mountain. The tall pines and hemlocks seemed to stretch into the sky. The oaks and maples were still clinging to some of their vibrant red, orange, and golds, holding on to autumn as long as they could.

There would be two days of nothing, lots of time to slowly tick by, but for the Marrino brothers, it didn't get much better than the big woods and a few steaks on the grill, whether or not any of them bagged an eight-pointer.

They were just turning off the road and heading down the long driveway to the cabin when Paul slammed the brakes. "Damn!" he yelled. "You see that?"

His brothers looked to where he was pointing at the window, at a huge buck leaping out from the brush just ahead of them.

Roy watched intensely as the big deer moved away in strong, graceful leaps. "Man, that's a ten-point buck!" He smiled. "I just hope we didn't scare him off for good."

They jumped out of the truck to get a better look. After a few minutes, they calmed down enough to start unloading their gear. Paul and Roy started teasing each other about who would ultimately be able to tag the big deer. For Rob, it was fun just to listen to his brothers carrying on, and he could do little but laugh at the two of them and their comebacks.

By the time they finished unloading the truck, the sky was fading into dark purples and grays, and the wind was picking up, carrying little white flakes of snow.

"It's gonna be a cold one by morning, boys," Paul said, looking up at the setting sun. "Might have a few snow squalls tonight."

Rob looked out at the horizon; the sky was becoming overcast, filling with dark gray clouds. "You're right, man. I can feel it too. It smells like snow in the air, more than just these few flurries."

Roy smiled. "Let's get inside and get that fire started. I'm damn cold already."

The brothers had been up in the mountains enough to know what Mother Nature was up to, and they'd learned long ago from their father to pack their gear right. "You don't take the right gear, you're gonna be freezin' your butts off," he'd told them. "Ya best have warm boots, heavy socks, hats, gloves, hand and foot warmers... It gets mighty cold by dawn in the mountains this time of year."

They finished unpacking in record time, and before long, they had a nice fire roaring in the wood stove. The rustic wood cabin was cozy and comfortable. It had a few bedrooms with a loft and lots of windows that allowed them to enjoy the view.

After dinner, the brothers took their seats around the fireplace, talking and watching hunting videos.
Rob opened his bottle of brandy and proposed a toast. "Gentlemen, here's to a good hunt...at a special place." They all clinked glasses, then took a sip of the fine blackberry brandy that he was happy to share.

Paul smiled at his brother. "Ya know, Rob, sometimes, I wish I could be like you. I mean, you get to travel around, and you're not tied to the same job day after day. I know you can't talk about it much, but it must be exciting."

Rob smiled. "Man, that's really weird, 'cause sometimes I wish for some of the things you guys have—a wife and family and more time to enjoy our nice place we have up here."

After they all had a good laugh, Roy added, "Listen, guys, that's why we come up here every year. This year, though, you're both gonna really wish you were me, 'cause I damn sure guarantee you I'm gonna nail that big buck we just saw. Y'all ain't got a chance." He said with another grin, then took another swig of his brandy.

The whole trio burst out laughing and teasing each other about who was ultimately going to get the buck. Rob poured them another round of the warming liquid, and the brandy began to take effect on the brothers as they relaxed by the fire.

"So, Rob, how is the Army life treating you? Have you seen any action lately?" Roy asked.

Rob lit his cigar and smiled at his brother. "You know what they say, brother. It's a dirty job, but somebody's gotta do it, and the pay is good. Not only that, but in another ten years, I can retire. I'll get a regular job and still collect a nice check from Uncle Sam every month on top of it."

"You can join the Carpenters Union and work with me," Roy added as he lit his cigar.

Rob grinned at him. "Thanks, bro. I'm not sure what I'm gonna do, but I may take you up on that. For now, I get to work with some good people and help our country. It's mostly security operations, but things are changing for the worse, I'm afraid. More and more, we find ourselves dealing with terrorism and the coming Jihad, their so-called Holy War."

Paul listened intently, trying to understand the meaning and brevity of his brother's words. *Why would the terrorists call it a Holy War?* He thought.

Rob's smile faded quickly. He took another sip of brandy, then continued, with a more serious tone to his voice, "Listen, guys... Believe me when I tell you there's a silent war going on out there. It's a war against terror and the evil darkness that is growing among them. My unit was on a covert mission in the Middle East this year. We heard a huge explosion in a nearby town. We eventually came to find out that one of them terrorists had blown himself to hell, right there in the marketplace. It was a bloody mess! Woman and children massacred, pieces of bodies everywhere… Damn, it made me sick! Those monsters hate anyone who isn't like them, who doesn't believe like they do, and they'll kill in a heartbeat. They live a totally distorted way of life." The room went silent for a moment, and Paul and Roy weren't sure what to say.

Rob's smile returned at he continued, "We are the light of freedom, though. We are there to ward off that darkness. You, me, and all of us need to be strong to keep that light shining."

Roy tried to imagine the horrors his brother had been through, but he couldn't even fathom it. "To hell with those bastards! It's time for you to relax and do some hunting."

Paul raised his glass. "To freedom's light! May it burn forever!"

After another round of the warm liquid, they were entirely relaxed, even yawning and stretching. Before long, it was time to turn in, they had to be up before dawn if they were going to make it to their tree stands before first light.

That night, Rob fell asleep with thoughts of settling down on his mind. He dreamt of having his own home, maybe sharing it with Ashley if she would have him. It wasn't long, though, before the aroma of brewing coffee stirred him from his slumber.

Paul was always up first, but the other two managed to crawl out of bed before the sun was even up, and everyone helped make breakfast. After a satisfying meal of hot grits, bacon, and scrambled eggs, they layered themselves in warm clothes and gathered their gear.

Rob carefully withdrew his new muzzle loader from its case and smiled as he examined it. The gun fit him like an old glove.

Just outside the house, Paul waited for his brothers. When they finally came out, armed and suited up for a hunting trip, he pointed to the woods. "Listen, guys… You already know where we're headed. Let's just keep quiet as we go in, and remember that we need to meet back here at ten a.m."

They trekked along the main trail, careful not to lose their footing in the expected light dusting of snow and ice. Soon, the three brothers were entirely separated, and each headed off in a different direction and disappeared into the cold, dark woods.

Using his small flashlight, Rob found his marker and headed through the pines, toward his tree stand. The cold air had a little bite to it, one that nipped at him even through his several layers of clothes. The leaves and snow and other forest debris crunched underfoot, so he tread as lightly as possible while he searched for his hunting spot. It took a while, but his flashlight soon glistened upon the metal frame of it. He made quick work of scampering up the tree and got everything set up, positioning himself and his body just right on the small perch. Then, he huddled against the tree and waited.

Not much noise broke through the stillness of the predawn night except the creaking and moaning of the big oaks, rustled by the occasional cold draft of wind. After a while, Rob really started to feel the bitter cold creeping in, so he poured himself some hot coffee from his thermos.

At last, the sun woke up to the east, breaking out of the clouds and bathing the woods in morning colors. Orange and gold streams of light filtered through the treetops, and the woods gradually came to life.

Somewhere in the distance behind him, Rob heard something. After listening a bit more closely, he surmised that it was the honking of geese in flight, growing ever louder. Suddenly, the air around him began to stir, as the big birds flew overhead, still honking and beating their wings in unison as they moved into the golden light of the rising sun. For Rob, it was like a scene from a beautiful painting. The crimson glow of the autumnal leaves and the graceful flight of the geese into the golden glow of the rising sun was majestic, like an unforgettable work of art. That moment, as he watched the formation fade into the horizon, was what those trips were really all about for him.

Next, Rob sensed some movement below. Rather than his quarry, the big buck, he spotted an enormous gray squirrel scampering in the brush, retrieving acorns and filling its cheeks. A few sparrows were fluttering about, chirping in the trees, but he saw no sign of a deer, even when he scanned around through the powerful scope on his gun.

In spite of his boots and more than one pair of wool socks, his feet and toes were beginning to tingle with coldness. The wind seemed to be picking up a little, so he decided to move to a little clump of trees just at the edge of the field ahead of him. Rob slowly made his way to the spot and discovered a perfect little nook to hide in; a place where the cold wind would no longer assault him. It was so comfortable, in fact, that after a while, he found himself sporadically dozing off; the hot coffee he'd slurped down in abundance had done nothing to stifle the effect of the brandy the night before and the early-morning wake-up call, even earlier than those military bugles.

Rob jumped with a start when he finally saw it, a huge buck, scuffling around behind him and to his right. He slowly swung his rifle to his shoulder and waited for a clear shot. The gun jumped, letting out a cloud of smoke as the *boom* echoed through the woods. The large animal looked in his direction for a moment. Then, to Rob's surprise, it just bolted across the open field, a blur of brown fur, and jumped into the woods.

"Damn it!" Rob yelled to himself, looking down at his gun in stunned disbelief. "How could I have missed? That shot musta been no more than forty yards!"

The wind continued picking up, blowing little puffs of snow from the branches every now and then as a defeated Rob followed the trail toward the house. It felt good to walk, and the momentum helped him warm up. Even his cold feet and aching toes began to feel a little better. When he finally reached the clearing, he looked toward the cabin. Outside the back door were his brothers, sitting on the deck, with steaming coffee mugs in their hands.

"Hey," Paul said as Rob approached. "I heard that shot. Was that yours?" he asked, handing his brother a fresh cuppajo.

Rob smiled sheepishly. "Yeah, man, I still can't believe I missed. It was a nice buck."

The brothers sat on the deck and talked for a while, slurping down more than their fair share of hot coffee.

A short while later, Rob happened to look down at something. There, lying on the step was a single fifty-grain black powder pellet. He picked it up and looked at it curiously for a moment before it hit him. "Look, guys! Can you believe it? I must have dropped this when I was loading my gun this morning." Even before Rob finished talking, he began to regret that he'd said anything.

Paul smiled. "Man, no wonder you missed that deer. You only had half a load."

Rob stared at the pellet and shook his head. "Damn. Now that I think about it, the gun didn't feel right when it went off."

Roy struggled to hold back his laughter. "Damn, Rob. Ya know, you're the only guy I know who goes hunting half-loaded!"

All three of the brothers had a good laugh about it, even Rob. Embarrassed as he was, even he had to admit that the oversight was hilarious.

During lunch, the guys rubbed it in really good. Rob wished he had put the damn pellet in his pocket, but it made him feel a little better to know it had nothing to do with his aim or his judgment.

It was only two thirty in the afternoon, but the sun was already low on the horizon as they made their way back to their tree stands. There seemed to be more clouds gathering, and the wind had stiffened a bit.

Rob didn't tell his brothers that he had found a better spot on the ground, since he knew they had put a lot of work in setting up the tree stands. He found the narrow trail and followed it to the stand, then headed farther down to his secret spot by the fields of winter wheat. The woods were quiet, except for the squirrels, busily gathering acorns from the big oaks. It was such a peaceful sight as Rob looked at the woods, aglow in the golden light of the setting sun. As he sat there, he thought about his brothers' words the previous night, about freedom's light, and it was nice for him to sit and enjoy it.

Soon, after no more deer sightings, Rob was back on the trail, heading for the cabin, just as the shadows of the coming night began to creep through the canopy of trees. As he walked, the *boom* of a rifle shot echoed through the woods. Instinctively, Rob dropped to the ground. He realized one of his brothers may have taken a deer, and he was right. From somewhere in the distance, Paul yelled out for help. When his brothers found him, they were happy to see that he had bagged the big buck after all. Rob and Roy searched for a tree branch large enough to carry it, and they worked together and slowly lifted the 250-pound animal and carried it back to the cabin. Regardless of who took the winning shot, they all celebrated; there would be plenty of venison to share with the whole family that year.

The next morning, before they set out again, the brothers partook of their traditional toast. Paul had the honors and raised his glass first. "Gentlemen, here's to another good year for the family, I pray we end up back here every year to spend some time together and do some good hunting."

It was a long ride back down the mountain, and Rob got an earful of jokes and teasing about his half-load. He silently prayed that he would be the one to get the big buck the following year. He had to; it was his only way out.

Chapter 3

Home

Time moved on. It was the first day of September, 2001. Rob was on his way back from a long, intense desert training mission. He had asked for a few weeks of downtime and was looking forward to being back home and spending time with Ashley. His plane landed at Newark Airport and taxied to the gate, and Rob found his way through the busy terminal to the baggage claim where he picked up his gear. He found his way outside, to the transport area, where he spotted Ashley's blue Chevy heading his way.

As soon as she threw the car in park, she jumped out with a broad smile on her face and ran to him.

Rob smiled back at her. "I missed you, baby!"

Ashley pulled him close. "I missed you too. You look so nice in your uniform."

Rob's grin broadened; he was so happy to feel her warm embrace again.

Quickly, they loaded up his bags and pulled out of the busy airport.

"You hungry?" Ashley asked with a smile.

"Starving. They sure don't feed people much on flights these days. Breakfast sounds mighty good to me," Rob replied. "Let's go to that little restaurant by the condo."

"Sounds great to me," Ashley replied as she pushed her long, blonde hair away from her face. She pulled off the turnpike and drove toward downtown Jersey City. The distant outline of Manhattan came into view as they found a parking spot by the restaurant. They were quickly seated and placed their orders right away.

Rob sipped his coffee as he stared into Ashley's stunning, blue eyes and took her by the hand. "You know something? You look better every time I see you. I don't have to report back to duty for two weeks, and I wanna spend most of it just with you."

Ashley's face brightened as she stared at the handsome man, lost in his warm, hazel eyes. She loved everything about Rob, from his dimpled chin and his high cheekbones to his tight, strong body and his funny smile. She could feel her nipples tighten; she was so hot for him.

Breakfast arrived rather quickly, and they ate hungrily. They talked about Ashley's new job, her promotion to assistant manager at Chase Financial in the city.

After breakfast, they went back to their condo and began to unpack. It wasn't long before they were locked in a frantic struggle to get their clothes off. The couch would have to do, for they didn't even make it to their bed. They'd missed one another so much, and they simply couldn't keep their hands to themselves.

Later in the evening, they did find their way to the bed, and it was a long while before they managed to make their way out of it. Ashley took a shower as Rob began to prepare dinner, salad with two juicy steaks.

Fresh from her shower, Ashley poured the wine as they sat down at the kitchen table to enjoy dinner and the view of the city lights from the windows.

On the other side of the globe, in the remote mountains of Afghanistan, Taliban leaders were putting the finishing touches on their hideous, maniacal plan. Through their twisted webs of communication, word came that everything was finally falling into place, almost ready to go. The tall, bearded one milled about the gathered crowd, congratulating them for a job well done, then sent out the final command. America was occupied by fanatical terrorists, bloodthirsty, hate-blinded killers walking her streets, just waiting to make their move. It was just a matter of time before the murdering began.

The next morning, Ashley was the first to awake and quietly slipped out of bed. She stood there for a moment, looking at Rob. She considered waking him, but decided to leave him to enjoy his peaceful, hard-earned slumber. She went to the kitchen to put on the coffee and make some breakfast.

Rob woke to the robust aroma of the percolating coffee pot and did a double-take to look at the clock on the wall. *How in the hell did I sleep in so late? I never do that!* Slowly, he sneaked down the hallway, toward the kitchen, and peeked around the corner. What a sight he saw, Ashley cooking as she danced around to the music blaring from her CD player, in nothing but her little black bra and panties. Rob could feel the heat growing inside him as he slowly sneaked up on her, getting as close as he could before he burst out laughing.

Ashley jumped in surprise. "Oh! Rob, you-you scared the hell outta me!"

"I'm so sorry, baby. I-I just couldn't help myself. You look so good!"

Ashley pulled him into a tight embrace. "You're a bad, bad boy," she teased, putting her housecoat on. "Now sit, and let's have some breakfast."

Rob had other ideas about how they should start their day, but he didn't want breakfast to get cold, so the two sat by the window and dug into their French toast and fried pork rolls.

Ashley smiled. "How about we go for a trip into the city today?"

"That sounds like fun," Rob replied. "We can go to the park and take the ferry across."

Ashley beamed, licking a speck of sticky syrup from her lips. "That'd be great. Let's get moving."

In northeast America, a group of twisted, evil terrorists waited, with murderous intent on their minds. They gathered at a predetermined location awaiting final word, their go-ahead to split up and move to what would be their final positions. Months of training and planning were behind them, and they would willingly sacrifice themselves. The murdering terrorists would die as so called martyrs. They would be rewarded on the other side, for showing America and the rest of the world just how vulnerable they truly were.

Rob and Ashley pulled off the busy highway and found their way to Liberty State Park, where they pulled into the parking area to catch the ferry. Rob purchased their tickets. The weather was a little cool, but the sun was starting to break through the clouds. Soon, they boarded the ferry and took their seats in the front, where they enjoyed the view of the Hudson River and the cityscape.

Ashley cuddled close to Rob. "The water looks nice and calm for a change," she said as the seagulls glided along the rippling surface while the ferry picked up speed.

"I love it out here," Rob said with a grin.

"Me too," she said. "How about we go down to the seaport and stop by to see my parents?"

"Sure. Why not?" Rob replied. "It'll be a nice walk down, and we can stop by that pub that makes those great sandwiches."

It wasn't long before the ferry pulled up along the dock at Battery Park. The driver tied up the boat and opened the gate. Rob and Ashley disembarked, and they walked toward the plaza at the Trade Center. As they walked, Rob couldn't help but look up at the massive towers that seemed to stretch into the clouds. Ashley pulled out her camera and took some pictures as they walked around the plaza, down toward the seaport. She decided to peruse one of the little shops while Rob relaxed with a newspaper.

Eventually, the couple reached the little pub. Since it was such a nice day, they requested a table outside. Rob was pleasantly surprised when their food quickly arrived; his pastrami sandwich was so thick he had a hard time getting his mouth around it. Ashley couldn't help giggling at him when his lips were glossed over with yellow mustard.

After lunch, Rob and Ashley made their way down to the seaport and found the bakery her parents owned. As soon as they stepped inside, Rob's nostrils were greeted with the rich, enticing aroma of fresh-baked bread and coffee. The sweet-smelling establishment was quite a lot bigger than it looked from the outside, and the oak-plank walls and flooring gave it a homey feel.

Ashley's mother, Maria, smiled at them as she walked around from behind the counter. She gave her daughter a big hug and said, "You two look so nice together. It's good to see you! Please come sit…and have some coffee."

Rob and Ashley sat at one of the small tables for two as Maria brought over a pot of fresh coffee and a plate of assorted Italian pastries. They sat for quite a while, talking and enjoying the delicious desserts; Rob somehow made room, even though he was still full of his sandwich from lunch.

Ashley glanced at the clock on the wall. "Rob, we've gotta get going, or else we're gonna miss the ferry."

That said, they said their goodbyes and headed back up toward the park. Luckily, they got there just in time to catch the last ferry. It was almost dark by the time they made their way home.

Back at home, Rob smiled as he stretched out on the couch. "I'd like a nice steak tonight…and maybe some of that good wine you always get from your mother."

Ashley jumped on top of him. "Is there anything else you desire, master?"

Staring into her eyes, Rob muttered, "Forget the steaks," and they instead ate a very late snack of bread, wine, and extra-sharp cheddar cheese after yet another romantic tryst.

Chapter 4

The Unthinkable

The morning of September 11, 2001 was crisp and clear. Paul was already thinking about the start of the hunting season as he took the turnpike to head east toward Secaucus. His mind was also on his job at the accounting firm. As he started across the top of the bridge, though, his attention was drawn to an unbelievable scene, so much chaos that he could do nothing but stop the car and stare in horrified awe.

Other cars were pulling over, and people were yelling and pointing from every direction, staring at the city from across the Hudson.

Is that... Oh my God! The Towers! Paul's mind scrambled, trying to comprehend what his eyes were seeing as he stared at the thick, black smoke billowing from the upper floors of the Trade Center.

"Planes! Planes!" a young woman screamed. "They said it on the radio! Oh my God! Planes have crashed into the Towers."

Within seconds, traffic was at a standstill, and there was terrified silence for a brief moment before a man yelled, "My wife works there!"

Paul made his way through the crowd, toward the distant city. It was slow-going, and by the time Paul managed another quarter-mile or so, everyone in every nearby office was huddled around a monitor or TV set, watching the grim report that one of the Towers had collapsed from the impact. Before long, it became apparent that it was no accident, that it was murder on a mass scale. Everyone watched in horror and disbelief as the second Tower collapsed. *"There is a terrible darkness growing,"* Paul remembered his Brother Rob saying so prophetically. *"The war against terror is here."*

About twenty-five miles from the city, in Carteret, New Jersey, Paul's brother Roy was on a job assignment at a glass plant. He was part of a crew of millwrights tasked with installing a huge production line. They were just about out of back iron pipe, so Roy headed for the supply yard to have a smoke and pick up more.

Outside, the crisp air reminded him that hunting season was just around the corner. *I've gotta give my brothers a call this weekend*, he thought.

As he moved closer to the storage area, he noticed a group of workers way up on the batch elevator platform. When he glanced up again, he saw them waving him over. Roy hurried up the ladders, traversing the ninety feet ascension as fast as he could, worried that something was broken or someone was hurt. "What's up, guys?" he asked when he stepped on the platform a few minutes later. Everyone was too shocked to answer, but when he looked around, he immediately saw why. He was too overcome with emotion to speak for a moment, but when his mouth could finally move again, he cried, "Oh my God! What the hell happened?"

Everyone just continued staring at the Towers, two structures burning in the distance, with billows of black smoke billowing in the breeze, polluting the sky and covering the city in ashes.

Finally, one of the workers blurted, "Freaking planes! They say it was two airplanes! Can you believe that shit?" Roy shook his head, stared at the carnage for a minute more, then scrambled down to tell the rest of the crew.

Back in the plant, they huddled around the radio, listening to the horrific play-by-play of the Towers collapsing. It was decided among them that a half-day of work was in order. Those who had loved ones who worked in the city left work immediately.

A couple of hours later, on the ride home, Roy remembered his brother's words: *"We must be strong, to shine the light of freedom against the darkness."*

The streets of New York City were a mix of shock and confusion. Police, firefighters, paramedics, and countless brave volunteers rushed into harm's way, hoping to help save lives. Unfortunately, some lost their own in the firestorm and debris as the Twin Towers came crashing to the ground. Hordes of terrified people ran and screamed, smothered in the ensuing dust storm. Slowly, they began to wander haplessly down the hazy streets and find their way to safety.

That September day, which had started out like any other, turned out to be one of unimaginable, unpredictable suffering and sacrifice, impossible to comprehend for the victims and their families and the world at large.

The cowardly enemy dealt a blow to weaken the will of the Americans, and everyone in the nation felt the terror, but began to rally to the aid of the injured Big Apple. The victims on the ground and in the air moved the nation closer together. Somehow, the people of

NYC slowly came out of their nightmare, stronger than ever. Despite the fear and horror felt on that sad terrible day, the United States pulled through, but that shock and grief gave way to a grave, burning anger, with one thought reigning in everyone's mind: *How could they do this to us?*

News broadcasts showed evil terrorists celebrating in the streets, as if the felling of the mighty Towers was a victory for them, burning the American flag with glee on their faces. The great Stars and Stripes, the Star - Spangled Banner America's forefathers had fought and died for, was blatantly disrespected and desecrated on foreign soil. Those cruel celebrations ignited a strong feeling of hatred, but they also sparked a deeper patriotism and pride, one that had not existed in the States since *Desert Storm* so many years earlier. Freedom's light continued to shine, burning even brighter.

Across the Hudson River, just west of the city, Rob and Ashley slept in late. They'd been up most of the night, as their passion for each other seemed to be as insatiable as ever. Rob always missed being home with the love of his life, and they had not been together for over three months. He called Ashley as soon as his leave cleared, and she was thrilled that her job at a big financial firm in the city gave her the flexibility to spend time with him.

Rob was interrupted from his peaceful sleep by the ringing and vibrating of his phone. He reached over Ashley to grab it, and what he heard coming from the other end of the line froze him, words that took some time to sink in: "Eagle's Claw," the recording repeated over and over.

Rob put the phone down. "Damn it! Ashley, honey, you need to get up, sweetie," he said, gently nudging her.

Ashley was slow to wake but realized something was dreadfully wrong, as soon as her sleepy eyes landed on his distressed face. "Rob, what is it?"

"Something bad has happened," Rob replied, frantically searching for the TV remote. "I need to see the news. There's been…some kind of major terrorist event," he said.

"Another one of those wars overseas?" she asked naïvely.

"No. Here, Ash. It happened here. Where is that damn remote?"

"Here!?" she asked, aghast and holding a hand over her mouth in shock. "As in the U.S.?"

"As in New York City, babe." I just got the call. The whole country's on Priority One Cen-Com Alert. I've gotta contact Command within the hour."

After they located the remote on the floor near the nightstand, the two of them sat on the bed, silently watching and listening in disbelief to the nonstop reports. The World Trade Center, the Twin Towers, had collapsed, bathing Manhattan in a thick layer of ash and smoke.

Ashley got up and ran to the window to look at the cityscape in the distance. "Oh my God!" she said, turning away. "I-I can't believe this."

Rob stood behind her, watching the drama unfold, shaking his head, and staving off tears. *How dare they attack us? So many innocent people…and now they're just gone.*

"My family!" Ashley suddenly screamed, with rivers of tears rolling down her cheeks. "Oh my God, Rob! They're over there, in that city. Gimme my cell phone."

Rob did his best to calm her down as she dialed the phone with shaky fingers. "Listen, Ashley, I'm sure they're okay. The seaport is far enough away, but the phone lines may be out. Try their cells instead of the landline."

After several more attempts, Ashley's face lit up. "Daddy? Are you all right?"

"Yes, honey, we're all okay, but we're shocked, to put it lightly. We're staying inside for now. There's a whole lotta commotion going on in the streets, with police and sirens and flashing lights everywhere. I don't think I've ever seen so many fire trucks in one place."

"Good, Dad," Ashley said, her voice trembling. "Just stay inside…and stay safe." Relieved that Ashley's family was okay, Rob sat back down to watch the news as her call continued. Ashley hung up a few moments later and walked over to sit next to Rob. "Thank God they're okay…for now."

"I knew they would be," Rob said, offering her a consoling smile.

As they watched the repeated video of the planes crashing into the two unsuspecting Towers, Ashley put her head on Rob's shoulder and asked, "How, Rob? How could anyone do something like that to all those innocent people? Why?" Her eyes filled with more tears as Rob tried to comfort her.

"I don't know, baby, but all we can do right now is hope and pray for the victims."

It took her some time, but Ashley finally composed herself and decided to take a shower. This time, it was

Rob who put the coffee on and whipped up breakfast for the two of them; she always loved his scrambled eggs and cheese with rye toast.

As he carried the food to the table, Rob listened to the TV. The news seemed to be getting worse and worse as time went on. Finally, he had enough and turned it off.

The two ate, mostly in silence until Ashley asked, looking into Rob's hazel eyes, "Do you really have to leave right now? I'm afraid! Please, Rob, I don't want you to go. If anything happened to you, I-I don't know what I'd do," she pleaded with a sniffle.

Rob could sense her love for him as he looked back into her beautiful, blue eyes. He pulled her close. "I will always be here for you, so don't go worrying yourself about it. The good Lord will take care of me. I'm just so damn angry at those terrorist bastards that I could rip their fucking heads off. Damn, I wish they wouldn't have gotten away with this shit. Still, I have to do my duty, Ash, to call in and report back to Command. Hell,

I need to do something. Now more than ever, our country needs us to be strong."

Ashley's mood seemed to lighten a bit. "You're right, Rob. Make your call, and I'll start packing your things. You're the bravest man I know."

"I'm just doing my job, honey."

"And the humblest," she said with a grin before she walked out of the kitchen.

Rob grabbed his cell phone and went out on the balcony for some fresh air, though he wasn't sure how fresh it would be as he stared at the huge cloud of smoke drifting over the city. It took several attempts to finally get through to Command, but in a short time, his orders were barked to him. He was to drive to an airbase located on the outskirts of Washington DC. Everything was on lockdown, and no flights were allowed in American airspace. Rob was ordered to report to Central Command 1, where he would await further instructions. He was sure the rest of his team was already on their way. He wondered what their new assignment would be, and he prayed he would have the chance to take some revenge on the evil souls who had killed so many.

Since Ashley had most of his things packed, Rob took a few moments to jump in the shower.

"I've gotta make sure you're nice and clean," Ashley suddenly whispered in his waterlogged ear as she sneaked into the shower behind him. In spite of the world crumbling around them, in that moment—a blissful collision of hot water, soap, rubbing, and kissing—nothing else existed.

After that exciting send-off, they shared some coffee, then walked together to Rob's car. Large gatherings of neighbors were scattered about, all talking about the happenings of the day, many pointing at the smoke rising from the bewildered and heartbroken city.

Rob unlocked his car and popped the trunk, then pulled Ashley close. "Please stay out of the city for now. Let things settle down a little."

Ashley smiled. "I will…and please call as soon as you can. You know I'm going to be worried sick."

Rob finished loading his gear and jumped in the car. He opened the window and gave her a soft kiss.

"Rob," she said, offering him a half-smile and biting her lip nervously, "please try to be careful out there. I will pray for you and your team."

He smiled back at her. "Don't worry, babe. I'll be back before you know it."

Ashley waved goodbye as he pulled away from the curb, then turned to walk back into her apartment. *What now?* She thought, trying to keep herself from having a meltdown. She decided her best course of action was to call in to work, to find out what was going on. Then she had plenty of prayers to say while she waited to hear from Rob and to have a chance to see her family in the city.

Chapter 5

Drums of War

Traffic was unbearably heavy on the way to the turnpike, so much so that it took Rob almost twenty minutes to get on the road that led to the toll booth, then another twenty to get his ticket. To the east, he could still see the huge clouds of gray smoke wafting up from the damaged city. He accelerated as he merged onto the highway and finally reached a tolerable cruising speed. Once he was away from the city, traffic eased a bit, and that gave him a chance to clear his head and really think about what had happened.

"Those damn cowards," he fumed, punching his steering wheel as his anger swelled inside him. "Fucking terrorists!" His experience in the Middle East during *Desert Storm* gave him a good idea about the most likely suspects for such a heinous, cowardly, arrogant act, and he assumed it was one of the Islamic extremists groups, perhaps funded by Iraqi or Afghan terrorists. "Probably just their sick, evil attempt at getting revenge for the butt-kicking we gave 'em in the war," he surmised.

He drove for some time, until he had to stop to gas up and stretch out a little. As he pulled back out to get on the highway again, he noticed someone standing at the end of the exit ramp, an older gentleman wearing what looked like a veteran's hat and Army fatigues, just staring out at the highway and holding a huge American flag. All the cars were slowing and waving at him, but he never moved and inch and just kept staring at the open road. As Rob passed by, a strange feeling overcame him. The man holding the flag looked like a scene right out of the Revolutionary War, when great men carried the flag to the marching beat of drums, urging them on in their fight for freedom. Rob felt the slow, encouraging beat of those drums as he drove on. He didn't realize it yet, but he was not alone; those same drums of war were slowly beginning to rise among the people. From the mountains to the plains, from coast to coast, all across the great land, the drums were sounding. A time of reckoning was coming for those who believed they could break the will and pride of the American people. Lives had been lost, but freedom would not be stolen from those who had fought so hard to earn it.

Back in Jersey, Paul left his job in Secaucus early. He couldn't help but notice the ominous clouds of smoke drifting from the city as he drove back over the bridge. He had stayed up late the previous night, immersed in the countless news reports broadcast on every channel, his heart wrenched with both anger and concern. He harbored a flaming fury for the twisted terrorists, who enjoyed killing innocent people, but he couldn't help but have compassion for the families of the victims, and he couldn't even begin to imagine the pain and suffering they were going through.

At the glass plant in Carteret, everyone was talking about what happened. Some of Roy's co-workers were missing, as they'd understandably taken some time off to locate family in NYC. Roy couldn't get over the newscast of the terrorists celebrating in the streets of the Middle East, and rage began to stir within him at the thought. *How could anyone even think of doing such a horrible thing?*

Later that night, after dinner, Roy prayed for all the people of New York. He wanted to go down to Ground Zero to help out, but he realized he had a job to do already, and he needed that job in order to feed his family.

Rob was on the outskirts of the DC area and Central Command when he saw a familiar sight on the horizon, another ominous cloud of smoke coming from the Pentagon. He knew about the attacks, as he had the radio on in his car, but the actual sight of it with his own eyes was something else entirely. Rob needed to do something to help. It calmed him a little to pray for the victims and their families, but he was a man of action and needed to take a more proactive approach. He didn't know what was going on, but there was one thing he knew for sure: *If I have the chance to strike back at those vile bastards, I'll jump at it in a heartbeat!*

He was familiar with the back roads, which allowed him to avoid the huge caravan of traffic. In the distance, he saw the red, white, and blue of several American flags. As he drove closer, he noticed a man on a horse, slowly trotting down the side of the road. The man was wearing a cowboy hat and holding a humongous flag, and he waved and smiled at Rob as he drove by. A sudden feeling of pride stirred within Rob, and by the time he finally arrived at Central Command late in the afternoon, his sense of patriotism was at an all-time high.

As Rob approached the Command entrance, he realized they had gone to great lengths to tighten security. There were barricades everywhere, and several heavily armed men surrounded the gatehouse. They stopped him before he even got close.

"ID please," a hard-faced guard demanded, looking none too pleased to see him.

Rob handed him his card, and the man walked into the guard shack with it. The security checkpoint took a while, as they examined his car and validated his identification.

"Sir, they are waiting for you in Building 3," the guard said, handing Rob's ID back to him.

The guards saluted Rob as he pulled the car past the gate and into the complex that was Central Command 1. A Jeep pulled up to the parking area, and Rob jumped onboard for his ride to the team meeting.

In the White House, the president addressed the nation, focusing his carefully worded speech on freedom, America, and the coming, inevitable fight against terrorism. It was very calming to hear his words about God and country. One thing he made undeniably clear was that there would be payback for the damage that had been done.

All U.S. military forces were placed on Code Blue High Alert, and what should have been done years before 9/11 was finally underway. Central Intelligence worked around the clock, gathering data. In the high-tech Cy-Com Satellite Surveillance Center, all available attention was focused on certain areas of the Middle East. Orders came from the top, demanding any and all Intel on terrorist groups around the world. The nation's top minds got to work, but everyone knew it would take a great deal of time to gather and analyze so much information.

Nevertheless, in a matter of days, the president and his team had the first report. Commander of Special Operations, General William H. Smithfield, finally received the call he was anxiously waiting for and learned that he was to report to a high-level meeting first thing in the morning. Smithfield was excited as he prepared for the meeting, knowing it might mean he could finally go to war on terror. Over the past few years, he had come to know more about the terrorists than most, and his elite Delta Force teams had completed several missions in the Middle East. This, however, would be something even bigger; he could feel it. The general had missed out on most of the action during *Desert Storm,* since he broke his leg in a skiing accident just prior, forcing him to watch it all unfold on CNN. *Not this time,* he thought to himself as he finished packing his briefcase. His key people were in place, and his best teams were preparing to go on his word. God willing they would soon be striking a blow on the evil terrorists who had dared to taint U.S. soil with the blood of its own innocent citizens.

The general awoke extra early the next morning, quickly showered, and fueled himself up with a good breakfast. Feeling full of energy, he turned on the news and waited for his driver. Finally, the big car pulled up, and he was on his way to the meeting.

Central Command consisted of a sprawling complex of buildings, all of which were a flurry of activity that morning. Cars arrived one after another, and security was intense. Inside the large meeting hall, General Smithfield mingled with some of his comrades, and it was clear that all the top brass of the major armed forces were involved. He recognized a few familiar faces among them as everyone took their seats along a pair of huge wooden tables. In the front, a large, digital display was mounted on the wall, with several laptop computers on a shelf below it.

Everyone recognized Secretary of Defense Blair Moreland as he arrived and made his way to the podium. The room grew quiet as Moreland looked around and began, "Ladies and gentlemen, I first want to thank all of you for making it here on such short notice. As you are aware, we have a very serious mission ahead of us. The president has asked me to begin this meeting with a moment of silence. Let us all pray for our fallen comrades and all the innocent lives that have been lost."

The room fell absolutely silent for a long moment, with most heads in the room bowed in prayer.

Moreland continues, "I have also been asked to show you a short video before we get started."

On his cue, the lights dimmed, and the digital screen came to life, revealing a large crowd of terrorists somewhere in the Middle East, celebrating, firing their weapons in the air, and proudly burning and stomping on an American flag. In another scene, which appeared to be in Afghanistan, more people were celebrating the American tragedy.

Those sick bastards, Smithfield thought, shaking his head in disgust as he watched the foreigners take joy in the senseless murder of thousands of innocent people.

When the room was illuminated again, the anger and tension in the air were almost tangible.

The secretary continued, "Each of you here can be assured of one thing. We will not let this behavior go unanswered. We will attack! The line in the sand has been crossed, and we will immediately begin planning to attack Afghanistan and the enemy. The terrorists believe this to be a holy war, and, by God, if war is what they want, war is what they are going to get…before they know it!"

Moreland walked around the table, glancing at each uniformed person in turn. "I will let you all get on with the details, and we will meet here every morning, until further notice."

As soon as the secretary of defense left the meeting, an endless array of maps and data was presented, and the countless hours of preparation commenced.

Smithfield felt a tap on his shoulder and looked up into the face of a young officer. "Yes?" he said, clearly annoyed by the interruption.

"Sir, the secretary would like to see you. Please follow me."

"Oh!" Smithfield almost jumped out of his seat. "It would be my pleasure," he replied, then quickly followed the enlisted man, into a plush, well-furnished office.

Secretary Moreland stepped forward and shook Smithfield's hand, offering him a smile. "Smithfield, I have heard a lot of good things about you. Please have some coffee."

Standing next to Moreland was an Air Force officer, along with an attractive woman he thought he might have seen before.

Moreland smiled. "Meet Commander Briggs and Special Agent Foster"

Smithfield shook hands with each of them, and they all filled their coffee cups as the secretary continued.

"General Smithfield, I have seen your file, and I must say I am very impressed. You seem to be holding the reins on some of our best available teams, the ones who can get the job done."

"Thank you, sir," replied Smithfield. "They are very anxious to prove themselves again."

Moreland moved closer to them and sat down. "I had a long talk with the president," he said. "As I mentioned earlier, we are going to attack. My problem is that our commander-in-chief is an impatient man. He wants something bad to happen to those bastards right now. Hell, the American people want their revenge so bad I can feel it in my bones."

"Sir, we are ready when you are," Briggs said assuredly.

Smithfield listened as the pretty woman in the suit added, "Gentleman, know that the CIA is at your disposal. The president has asked me to provide any and all intelligence that may be needed."

Moreland looked sternly at Briggs and Smithfield as he said, "Agent Foster and I have discussed this matter, and we already have a target. Our Intel is firm. There is a terrorist weapons facility that also serves as headquarters for some of their key people. Right here in this room, with the three of you, I have the intelligence and the expertise to reach out and touch them. What I need is a detailed plan, and I need it within the next forty-eight hours. The president and the American people are waiting. Lady and gentlemen, it's go time!" With that said, the secretary departed.

The others put on another pot of coffee and worked through most of the night before the plan took shape. There were still a few details to work out, but Smithfield felt good about it. When he left to return home, he was exhausted but excited, and he looked forward to meeting with his Delta Force team in the morning.

Chapter 6

Plans

The following morning, Rob and his comrades were up early and ate breakfast in the meeting area of Central Command. They had gotten word late in the night that something was underway, and Smithfield seemed excited.

The team, technically known as a Special Missions Unit, consisted of soldiers from the Delta Force Operations branch of the U.S. Army, one of the elite teams in the American military. Known by their codename, Light Force, they had been effectively working and training together for the past three years, and they had achieved some very lofty goals and completed missions thought impossible.

The six members of Light Force each came equipped with their own unique skills. Lt. Rob Marrino was at the lead. Sergeant Tex Martin was the weapons specialist, a tall, rugged Texan who always had a rather large blade strapped to his leg, as well as his legendary M60 machinegun by his side. Corporal Jim Moralez handled engineering and explosives, and he was a marksman of the highest caliber, especially with his special night-vision sniper rifle. Corporal Lee Adams was the communications specialist, and he carried the uplink and a standard M16. Last, but certainly not least were Josh Lee, the medical specialist, and Phil Takis, another weapons specialist. So that each man would always have a backup, all were trained to do the others' jobs; if one man was down, someone else could step up to fill in the gap, though the need seldom arose.

"Look at that horrible mess," Jim Moralez said as they watched the latest CNN reports at Ground Zero and the news about the flight that crashed in Pennsylvania. "My sister Rita works in that part of the city. I've been trying to reach her, but she's not answering her phone, and my parents haven't heard any word on her either." He slammed his fist on the table, his eyes full of hate as he continued, "If those bastards..." His words trailed off as he struggled to hold back angry tears. "I'm ready for this one, you guys—more ready than I've ever been for any damn thing."

The room went quiet for a moment as Rob sat next to Moralez and tried to settle him down.

Tex suddenly jumped up and pulled out his huge blade. "You fellas know what I want, what I pray for?" he asked, gripping the knife, his eyes burning with wrath. "Just me and that terrorist leader out there in the desert...or any man those cowards wanna put up to the challenge. We'll fight to the death in the sand dunes, damn it!"

Rob smiled at his friend and put his hand on his muscled shoulder as he tried to ease the tension. "Easy there, big fella. You'll get your chance. Hell, Tex, we all feel the same way, but we gotta stay sharp and focused, or we won't do anyone any good."

Adams, who was usually the quiet one, yelled in an uncharacteristic tone, "Oh, I'm focused all right. Yes, sir! I'm so damned focused it's killing me! I just pray for a chance to avenge my comrades."

"You know what really gets to me the most?" Rob asked, shaking his head. "That flight, the one heading toward DC. Those guys rushed the cockpit and crashed the plane before it hit its intended target. Can you imagine the balls that took, standing to fight even though they knew they were gonna die anyway? That was bravery at its purest form, giving their lives so others could live. I pray for them and for the chance to avenge all the victims of 9/11...as well as its heroes."

For a moment, the room silenced again. It did them some good to let their emotions out. Rob reflected back on the man with the flag, and the drums of war began to beat even stronger within him.

As the tension eased, the men began talking again, reminiscing about some of their prior assignments and the good times they'd had. Their reverie was broken when the phone rang.

"That was Smithfield," Rob told the others after he hung up. "He'll be here within the hour."

Back in the Cy-Com Center, one of the specialists was monitoring the satellite images when something drew her attention, an anomaly that demanded a closer look at the image in front of her. She carefully scanned it until she was sure of what she was seeing: There, in a remote area of northern Iraq, there was a rectangular area that did not quite seem to blend in with the surrounding geology. A section of flat ground extended out from the large rectangle, like some sort of roadway. She immediately notified her supervisor, Stan Gustan, and he hurried over to examine it himself.

"Hmm. The edges are too straight for that to be any sort of natural formation. I don't like it," Gustan replied as he traced out the outline of the rectangle with his pen. "Looks to me like somebody's trying to cover something up, and they aren't doing a very good job of it." He then turned to another specialist. "See if you can pick up this area from a different angle," he ordered, "then monitor the location and report back to me if you notice any changes."

Gustan entered his office and made a direct call to Secretary Moreland on the hotline to tell him about the image.

"Gather as much Intel as possible and bring it to Agent Foster's office first thing tomorrow morning," Moreland advised. "Also, commend your team for a good eye."

General Smithfield arrived at Central Command with Agent Foster, and both seemed to be in good spirits, considering the circumstances. Normally, the general would hand a mission off to a subordinate, but this time, he wanted to keep things under his control.

"Gentlemen," Smithfield said with a grin, glancing around the room at Light Force, "I have big news. We have been selected by the president to take an important strike at the enemy."

"Sir," Rob added, "That is the best news we could possibly get. We've been waiting and hoping this would be the case."

Tex smiled as he ran his finger along his big blade. "You can count on us, sir. Just tell us when we're gonna get this party started."

Agent Foster looked at the big Texan. "If all goes as planned, we will schedule launch within the next few days."

Smithfield laid out a huge map, and Agent Foster set up some charts. "This will be known as *Operation Firefly*, and your intended target is in southern Afghanistan. Light Force will go in first, and this will be a two-part assault on the terrorists and their command structure."

Agent Foster added, "We have firm data that the terrorists have an outpost there, next to a small airport. Our sources indicate that we have a very high probability of taking out the terrorist leaders, perhaps even the big man himself."

The general continued as he pointed at the map, "The team will fly to our airbase in Saudi Arabia for refueling, then set up and head for the target. You will be flown in by chopper, under the cover of night, and dropped off at a predetermined LZ." Smithfield paused, giving them a chance to take it all in, then continued, "Your mission will be to recon the area, infiltrate the outpost, and gather any information you can. When the mission is complete, or if anything goes wrong, you will withdraw. Use your uplink and call in for an airstrike on the facility. With God's help and your skills, we hope to smash those terrorists to pieces."

Rob could feel the intensity and confidence in the general's words, see the fire in his eyes. Everyone seemed eager to get started, and he couldn't blame them one bit, because he felt the same way.

Smithfield and his staff began going over the endless details of the plan, and the general broke into a smile as he picked up the phone. "How about we order up some coffee and sandwiches?" He asked. "Maybe some good ol' apple pie to go with it, shall we? I got a feeling it's gonna be a long night."

"Can't think of anything more American than planning an assault with some old-fashioned apple pie!" Rob said with a smile.

Chapter 7

From the Ashes

Back in New York City, the World Trade Center and the surrounding buildings had been reduced to an enormous pile of rubble. Mountains of steel beams, ash, and chunks of concrete lingered there, the dilapidated remains of commerce and lives once lived. The entire surrounding perimeter was enclosed by police barricades, and only qualified workers, firefighters, and emergency and rescue personnel were allowed even close to the sight.

Teams of rescuers were determined to find more survivors as they went about the grim task of carefully sifting through the debris. Volunteers came from everywhere to help the crippled city. Before long, it would be time to bring in an army of personnel and heavy equipment to begin the long process of clearing the site.

Ashley finally found her way into the city and was relieved to see the old neighborhood, still standing. Her friends and family were happy to see her again, and she was more than relieved to see them. She learned that it would be at least another two weeks before she had to return to work at the investment bank, as it was in the process of a temporary relocation, uptown and away from the tumult. Her parents insisted that she stay with them for a few days, as they had a big apartment with plenty of room.

Ashley spent some time at her parents Café Bakery, down by the seaport, helping to fill the takeout orders from workers headed to the disaster site. She met two firemen from New Jersey, as well as many others from the surrounding area; people and equipment came in from all over the country to lend a helping hand. In the wake of that bitter tragedy, even Ashley could feel that the American spirit was still alive and well. Everywhere in the city, people seemed to be pulling together. For their part, Ashley's father and some of the neighbors loaded up his van with free soup and sandwiches for the police and firefighters.

Later that night, Ashley went outside to enjoy a comforting cup of tea. She looked out at the skyline, all those twinkling lights in the distance, listening to the faint *hum* of machinery working overtime at Ground Zero. She thought of Rob and the last time they rode the ferry together from the Trade Center. It was difficult to imagine that it was all gone, and how she wished Rob could be with her. She prayed for him, but she still felt compelled to do more. She wanted to go down to the site, to see it with her own eyes, but she wasn't sure she could drum up the courage. *But if Rob is so brave, I can be too,* she told herself. *Maybe I can help somehow, in some small way.* She also prayed for the thousands of victims and their families.

A few nights earlier, Rob's brother Paul called, asking to talk to Rob.

"He's away…on another mission," Ashley told him.

"Oh, I figured he might not have left yet. Well, do you need anything?"

"No thanks," she answered. "I'm all right."

"Okay," Paul said. "Things are getting pretty crazy out there, Ashley. If you need anything—anything at all—let me know…and please let me know if you get any word from Rob."

"Will do," Ashley said, and she could sense the concern in Paul's voice as she hung up the phone.

In a remote area of northern Iraq, a group of terrorists were sleeping in the back of a large, makeshift airplane hangar. After months of endless labor, their work was almost done. Sitting under the hangar was a large passenger jet that had been stripped and fitted with extra fuel capacity. The aircraft was also loaded with over three thousand pounds of high explosives and several large canisters of orange-colored, highly toxic, poisonous gas. Their target was a major city along the eastern seaboard of the United States of America. All that was missing were the jet fuel and the pilots.

Back in the Cy-Com Center, it was almost midnight. Stan Gustan and his team had finished putting together an amazing display of images, including pictures of foot traffic and vehicles moving in and out of the rectangle.

Gustan had also finished his detailed report. He handed the locked briefcase to a special courier team for an early-morning trip to Central Command and was relieved that the vital information was on the way to the people who could do something about it. He had a bad feeling, and his instincts were usually right on par.

At the remote terrorist base, the last of the fuel trucks pulled in to top off the tanks of the jumbo jet. Another crew was busy making the final preparations on their version of a runway. The base was situated in a wide valley, between two large, rock-strewn mountains. The surrounding land was a forsaken, waterless desert, a place of endless, reddish-brown dust, soil, sand, and rock.

The terrorist leaders were in the final stages of their long-awaited and hideously evil plan. If everything proceeded according to that plan, the pilots would arrive soon, and the big jet could be airborne in two days.

Chapter 8

Deadly Intentions

Early the following day, Agent Foster made her way through security and entered the enormous Central Command Center. She stopped at the front desk to pick up her keys, then walked down the hallway to the break room for her usual cup of black coffee, along with a crispy, sweet donut. Fueled up with caffeine and sugar, she finally made her way to her office.

As she turned the corner, she spotted a man standing at her door, with a briefcase in hand. The messenger identified himself and handed over the gray metal case and the corresponding key.

Foster thanked him, then entered her office, locked the door, and immediately opened the case. She sipped her coffee as she studied the photos and read the report in disbelief. After a quick perusal, she picked up the briefcase and walked toward the elevator and up to the top floor to meet with General Smithfield.

Back at the Army base, Rob and his team were up early, having breakfast after their daily five-mile run. The day of packing up and getting ready for deployment had arrived, and everything had to be checked and double-checked, as any little problem could turn deadly if they weren't careful. Mistakes and malfunctioning equipment were simply not an option.

After breakfast, Rob led his team out of the mess area. They boarded a van for a ride across the massive base complex to the airfield. They pulled up to one of the large transport aircrafts and met with the flight crew, then began checking and packing their jump gear. The coming mission called for a high-altitude jump, as well as the absolute stealth of a night drop.

"Okay, guys, load your gear onboard and get set up," Rob commanded. "Our departure orders could come at any minute, and we have to be ready to haul ass!"

Tex smiled as he looked over the aircraft. "Jumping outta planes sure ain't my favorite way to begin a mission, but I'd do just about anything for a chance to get back at those bastards."

Josh added, "Oh, c'mon, Tex. If you're scared, you can hold my hand when we bail."

Everyone broke into laughter and continued loading their gear. A short while later, things were quiet, and there was no more joking around as they boarded the aircraft, fully focused on the mission ahead.

General Smithfield was at his desk when his secretary called and told him that Agent Foster was there to see him. "Send her in," he replied, wondering why she was there at such an early hour.

Foster walked through his door and set the briefcase on his desk. "Cy-Com just sent this to me," she said, with a grim look on her face. "I don't wanna believe my eyes, but the images are clear. Have a look, General." She then took a seat as Smithfield opened the briefcase and looked over the photos.

"What the hell? It looks like some kind of secret base or something. Look at the size of this rectangular area, and I sure don't like all that activity going on there. The images show what appears to be a large group of terrorists moving around. There could be anything inside that structure, maybe even a large missile."

The general picked up the hotline and immediately called Secretary Moreland.

Moreland was pouring himself a hot cup of coffee when his phone rang. "Who the hell calls a man before his first cuppajo?" he mumbled as he picked up the phone. He soon had his answer, for he recognized Smithfield's voice immediately, and the sense of urgency in it was undeniable.

"Secretary, sir, I'm afraid I just received some…rather disturbing Intel that you should see immediately. The terrorists are up to something big in northern Iraq."

"Where did this data originate from?" Moreland asked, with concern is his voice.

"It arrived from the Cy-Com Center, sir. They hand-delivered it to the Agent Foster this morning."

"Okay, but if it's as urgent as you say, we can't wait for you to drive up here," replied Moreland. "Have Cy-Com fax copies to our secure line at the Information Center immediately."

As soon as Moreland hung up, he dialed the direct line to the president to fill him in on the situation. The commander-in-chief instructed him to bring the Intel to the morning cabinet meeting. After his conversation with the president, Moreland called for his driver. He was escorted to his car and was on his way to the Information Center within five minutes.

Back at the airfield, Rob and his team were finished with their final preparations. They had just received word to stand down until further orders. Everything was set to go, and all they needed was a final command to depart.

Light Force jumped in the van for the ride back across the airfield, to their quarters. Rob watched other Delta Force teams by their transports, also preparing for deployment. He was glad it was going to be a team effort, and he was anxious to get going.

As soon as Rob arrived back at their quarters, there was a phone call for him. He picked up the line and immediately recognized the voice of his brother.

"I was thinking of you today," Paul said. "I hope you don't mind that I'm giving you a call."

"You can call me anytime, big brother," Rob said, glad to hear from him.

Paul continued, "Thanks. Anyway, how are you doing?"

"Things are busy around here right now, and I might be gone for a while. I wish I could say more, but... Well, I'm sure you understand. How's the rest of the family doing?"

"We're all okay," Paul answered. "Man, everyone's still talking about what happened, and they probably will be for a while. Can you believe this shit? Anyway, you know our prayers are with you, little brother."

"Thanks, Paul."

"Oh, yeah...Ashley called me last night. She said you had better ring her up, or else she's gonna kick your butt."

Rob laughed. "Thanks for the heads-up, bro. You know, with everything going on, I almost forgot to give her a call. Thanks for reminding me."

"You know I've always got your back, Rob."

The brothers talked for a few minutes, and after they hung up, Rob poured himself another cup of coffee. He then called Ashley, desperately hoping she was home to take his call. He missed her already, and the last thing he wanted was to worry her unnecessarily by not keeping in touch with her when he could.

Back in Iraq, the pilots finally arrived at the makeshift hangar. The terrorists celebrated those who'd so bravely taken the one-way flight to their so-called martyrdom. Afterward, the pilots began looking over the exterior of the aircraft, and then went inside to inspect the deadly cargo and make sure it was secure. In the cockpit, they began their pre-flight checks.

Before long, the massive jet engines came to life, and the terrorists cheered as the aircraft taxied out toward the runway. They were elated, and they knew it was too late for anyone to stop them now.

The pilot smiled, he slowly increased the throttle and moved the aircraft to its final take-off position. The pilot throttled up, but just as he released the brakes and began to gain speed, the engines flamed out, one of them billowing black smoke. Warning buzzers and flashing lights filled the cockpit. Frantically, the pilots scurried around the cockpit, their eyes wide with terror. The engines shut down, and the huge aircraft coasted to a stop in the middle of the runway.

Quickly, the terrorists disembarked and began towing the damaged aircraft back, to the safety of the hangar. As their luck would have it, our satellites were not in position to lock on to the jumbo jet, but for the time being, they were grounded. Some might have believed it was a sign that God was on the side of good, but whatever the reason, the broken plane was about to buy the Americans some time.

Moreland arrived at the Information Center and looked over the faxed images and report in disbelief. He stuffed them in his briefcase and headed to the cabinet meeting. After passing through security, he entered the meeting room and sat across from the president, who was smiling at him. Moreland passed the briefcase to the president. "Sir, we just acquired this data from Cy-Com."

The president looked over the pictures, and then looked up at Moreland curiously. "What do we have here?" he asked hesitantly, as if he wasn't sure he wanted to hear the answer.

Moreland stood and answered, "Sir, my gut instinct is that this is some kind of secret base. I fear the terrorists are hiding a missile system. We're not sure, but as you can see, someone went to a lot of trouble to keep that base concealed."

"I don't like this, Moreland, not one bit," the president said, his face etched with concern. "I don't like not knowing what we're dealing with." He stood and walked around the table. "If it is the terrorists, they are likely using this presumably secret facility to plan another attack. God only knows what they're housing there."

The photos were then passed around the table. Each cabinet member looked them over carefully, wincing and whispering as they did so.

Secretary of State Karen Stiles stood and spoke directly to the president. "Sir, we have to be careful about this. The photos don't provide proof of anything other than some kind of small military base in Iraq. We can't even prove that the people in the photographs are terrorists."

The discussion gradually turned into a heated debate, with remarks and opinions being thrown around and across the table, until the president intervened.

"Ladies and gentlemen, let us not forget that America has been attacked!" he interrupted, his voice loud and clear. "New York, the Pentagon... What's next? I don't know about the rest of you, but I'm not willing to wait around to find out. They caught us off guard, and people are dead because of it. We must be on the offensive from now on."

"But, sir—" Secretary Stiles tried to cut in.

Ignoring her, the president continued, in a stern voice that left no room for doubt, "A series of strikes is being organized as we speak. There is no other option. I want this so-called base checked out, up close and personal. If it is a terrorist hub, I want it destroyed, completely leveled."

The room grew silent for a moment as the president took his seat.

Defense Secretary Moreland excused himself for a moment and made a quick call to Smithfield. "We've got to get the ball rolling on this, ASAP," he said. "The president wants action."

"Understood," Smithfield agreed, then hung up the phone, realizing the mission had just been placed fully in his hands. He had the prestige and the power of the president behind him and the responsibility of an intricate mission to complete. Time was of the essence, and they had to make it happen. It might have been a daunting feat for most, but Smithfield was thrilled with the opportunity. Finally, he would have a chance to truly prove himself. He had been waiting for such an important mission for the duration of his career.

Immediately after hanging up with Moreland, Smithfield called and ordered his subordinates to arrange a meeting at Central Command. Everyone with any vested interest was to be in attendance, first thing in the morning. With the initial details out of the way, Smithfield left for some drinks at the officer's club.

The next morning, Rob was in his quarters when a call came through for him. He picked up the phone, certain it was Ashley, and he was happy to find that his guess was right. It felt good to hear her voice again.

"Hey, soldier boy," she said sweetly, "I've been waiting for you to call. How are you? What have you been doing?"

"I'm sorry, baby. I've been meaning to give you a call, but things have been busy as hell around here. I'm fine, but I miss you already. We're getting set for a mission. It may be a while before we can talk again, so I'm glad you called. How are you and things back home?"

"It's been hard dealing with what happened, but I'm okay." It took a moment for Ashley to find the words before she continued, "I spent some time in the city, with my parents. I took your advice and waited a few days before I went. Everyone's still pretty shaken up about it, and the place is a mess. It took me all day just to get there with all the commotion going on, but things have settled down a bit."

"That's good."

"Yeah. I think people will come around in time. It's just all so shocking, you know?"

"I can only imagine. I think it blew all our minds."

"I love you, Rob, and I'm so worried about you. I know I can't talk you out of doing your duty, but I will pray for you and your mission."

"Ash, I know it's hard, but please try not to worry so much about me. I love you, too, and I'll see you again, probably before you know it."

Rob and Ashley talked about home and the family for a while, before someone called out his name, needing his help with one thing or another.

"Do you have to go so soon?" Ashley whined.

"Yeah, sweetheart. I'm sorry, but I've gotta go. I'll call again as soon as I can."

Just as Rob hung up, the phone rang again, with an incoming call from Central Command, to inform him that the team was being put on high alert again. General Smithfield had ordered a mission review meeting in a few hours. Rob passed word to his team, and they rushed to prepare for the quickly upcoming meeting.

Back in the remote mountains of Iraq, the terrorist leader frantically paced around the aircraft, impatiently awaiting word as to how long the repairs would take. He was worried that his plan would be discovered and thwarted before he could launch his sinister attack. The mechanics had arrived from Baghdad hours earlier, and they were still working on the blown jet engine.

Finally, one of the so-called experts approached him, pushing burned-up engine parts on a tool cart. The main bearings and fuel lines were shot. "I am afraid there will be a delay," he told his leader. "We must locate and order replacement parts."

It was not good news for the leader of the terrorists, but unbeknownst to the people of America, it had bought them more precious time.

Chapter 9

Light Force

At Central Command, Rob and his teammates sat in the meeting room, awaiting the arrival of General Smithfield. He was sure it would be their final soiree before the big-time mission was underway, but Tex had bet him a twenty that it wasn't. The entire team was ready to go, and all were growing weary of waiting around.

Smithfield finally showed up, with a group of officers in tow. He instructed his assistant to set up the large computer display in the front of the room. Anyone who knew the general could tell by the spring in his step and the bright smile on his face that he was excited.

Everyone took their seats as Smithfield stood beside the display screen. He looked at Rob and his team and began, "Boys, there's been an important change in plans." He used his pointer on the display and continued, "It seems we have a new target here, in northern Iraq. This will be a very high-priority recon mission. We need to find out what the hell's goin' on at this location." As his assistant handed out some photos, mission details, and location coordinates, he went on, "Gentlemen, stealth, speed, and timing will be paramount here. My gut is telling me that these fiends are housing some sort of long-range missile system, and we all know they don't have good intentions. Your departure is set for 0500 tomorrow morning."

"Are we supposed to engage the enemy?" Tex asked, not bothering to disguise the hope in his voice.

"No, not unless it is unavoidable. Once you find out what's going on at the location, you must report back with the uplink. If it's what we suspect, we will launch cruise missiles to make a preemptive strike and wipe them out. I encourage all of you to get some shut-eye, fellas. You're sure as hell gonna need it." That said, the general dismissed Rob and his team. Smithfield took his seat with the other officers, and they began going over the endless details of the mission.

On the outskirts of an American airbase in Saudi Arabia, several Saudis were working on an oil rig when they noticed a large shadow moving toward them from the distance.

One of them looked up just in time to see what was causing the shadow. "Look! Look!" he screamed as he watched what he thought was some sort of spaceship gliding over them.

The rest of the oil rig crew stared, their mouths agape, then began jumping up and down with excitement. What they were actually looking at was a high-tech American B-1 super stealth bomber, gliding over the sand dunes and coming in for a touchdown at the American airbase. The bomber would be modified for the coming mission and the flight into Iraqi airspace. The oil rig crew watched in awe as the flying object whizzed through the sky and disappeared over the sand dunes, melting into the horizon and out of sight.

At Central Command, Rob and his team went over the details again and again, until each man felt confident. After that, they played cards and devoured some pizza, laughing and taking time to relax.

"I'm out," Rob said, throwing his cards down on the table when he lost yet another twenty bucks to Tex.

"C'mon, Rob! Just one more round?" Tex begged.

Rob stood, wearing a stern look on his face. "No way, buddy. The way I see it, you've gotta have an ace up your sleeve or something. Plus, I thought I saw you peeking at my cards."

The room suddenly went quiet, and the two men engaged in an intense stare-down. Finally, Rob smiled, and the whole room burst out in laughter; it was a good chuckle they all needed, it helped ease the tension.

Light Force would be well equipped for the mission, with the latest technology, GPS navigation units, night-vision headsets, and satellite uplinks. They went over the plan one more time, then headed to their quarters to get some sleep.

Everyone was resting peacefully in their bunks except Rob, disturbed by thoughts about the mission, as well as his wondering about the people in New York City. Stop, he told himself. We're ready. Everything's in place, all our gear is stowed on the C-140 transport that is sitting by the runway. He finally dozed off with thoughts of Ashley on his mind, hoping to catch a few sweet dreams before their 0500 departure.

The team was set to head to the American airbase in Saudi Arabia. From there, they would board the stealth bomber for a high-altitude jump to their target. It would be a night plummet into the remote mountains of Iraq, and not a soul would see them coming.

In northern Iraq, the terrorists were still waiting for the parts to repair their jet engine. The engine housing and other pieces were cleaned and ready for reassembly, but without the main bearings and fuel lines, the plane was little more than a dead duck in the water.

The group leader, Amwa Binfudi, was pacing again when one of his scouts came running down from his lookout. "*Haboob*! *Haboob*!" the man yelled, pointing at the horizon.

Binfudi and his comrades ran along the runway for a better look. They could see the vast clouds of dust stirring on the horizon, moving toward them.

Enraged, Binfudi screamed in disbelief. He stormed back to the aircraft and began barking orders, demanding that his men gather up the parts and close up the aircraft.

The wind began to pick up, and before long, it was so thick with reddish-brown, sandy dust that they found it difficult to see or even breathe. They hurried inside their quarters to wait out the dust storm, furious that their atrocious plan was delayed once again. As if it was not frustrating enough that the repairs were taking so long, it would now take even more time to clean out the aircraft engines from the swirling debris. Things were simply not working out in their favor, and Binfudi was beginning to wonder why.

Tex was the first one up, just before 0400, as excited as a kid on Christmas morning; he'd never been able to sleep well the night before a mission. He had a strange feeling about the coming mission, though, and he wasn't sure why. Alone in his bunk the night before, he'd said a quiet prayer for his team and their safe return. He wasn't always a praying man, but something about going to Iraq had him quite unnerved. Nevertheless, he was eager to get things underway.

The base alarm finally went off, and the rest of the team began sitting up in their bunks. Rob turned the lights on and found Tex just sitting there, staring at him with a Cheshire Cat grin on his face.

"Ya know," Tex teased, "you were snorin' somethin' wicked last night, buddy."

Josh added with a smile, "You got that right, Tex. For a minute there, I thought a buncha lumberjacks broke in here with their buzz saws."

Rob stretched out on his bunk. "Sorry if I disturbed your beauty sleep, boys. God knows you needed it," he said, grinning at Tex.

"How does that little lady of yours get any sleep at all?" Tex added with a smile. "Man, if you snore like that when we're out on location, I'm gonna stuff a sock in it."

After a round of laughs at Rob's expense, the team settled down, and everyone began to get dressed. They had to hurry through breakfast at the mess hall, then get down to business. It was going to be a long day, much longer than any of them realized.

General Smithfield walked down to the airfield and stood at one of the transports as his troops gathered in front of him. There were a total of eight teams, including Light Force, and they quickly fell into formation, waiting to board their respective C-140 transports for their ride to the American airbase in Saudi Arabia. He looked over his troops as he spoke. "You all have a mission to do, and you know your assignments, so I'll keep this short and sweet. Today marks the first day of payback time, and all of you are the chosen ones to collect on this debt. Strike down the evil terrorists. Show them no mercy for what they have done. Do your country proud, boys and girls…and make sure you all come back in one piece!"

Once his pep talk was over, the teams dispersed with quick precision boarded their transports. Tex was the first onboard theirs, followed by Rob and the rest of the team. As soon as everyone else piled in, the pilots closed the big doors and taxied toward the runway.

Smithfield and his staff stood by the runway and watched the big transports accelerate down the runway. The general stood at attention and saluted as he watched each plane lift off and disappear into the horizon; he prayed for their safe return. Once again, it was up to the troops to venture into harm's way and get the job done, and he had every confidence that they would do just that.

Across the United States, things were slowly getting back to some semblance of normal, even though the Americans knew life would never quite be the same again. High-level meetings were in progress in Washington, focused on a wide increase in homeland security, and all branches of the military were placed on high alert. The wheels were set in motion for a series of deadly strikes, an answer to the terrorists who had dared to take down the Towers.

Military reserve units were dispersed to patrol all major airport terminals. In New York City, the raw horror and shock was beginning to turn to anger and resolve. People from all over the nation came to their aid, to begin the tremendous task of cleaning up the area now known as Ground Zero.

In the other forty-nine states, people try to come to terms with and understand the cowardly attack on the innocent people of New York City. It was a rude awakening to just how vulnerable America was, and people were upset, fearful, and angry. Many turned to their faith and prayed for the victims and their families, and countless others volunteered their time and effort to help the people of the city in any way they could. Teams of workers began the enormous effort to clear the huge piles of steel and rubble that was once the World Trade Center.

In northern Iraq, the wind died down, and the raging curtain of dust finally dissipated, leaving the aircraft dusted with a film of reddish-brown dirt, as thick as a shag rug. Binfudi ran around the airline in a rage, screaming orders at his men, who were doing their best, undertaking the tedious, time-consuming task of cleaning the sand out of the jet engines. Other crews busied themselves with cleaning of the rest of the plane and clearing the piles of sand off the runway.

Soon, a Jeep came into view on the road leading to the base. The messenger pulled up to the hangar and reported to Binfudi the good news that the part for the jet engine had been located and ordered and was on its way. The clock was still ticking, but the terrorists had something to celebrate once again. Binfudi was especially anxious to get his flying bomb airborne, so he harshly ordered that everyone stop wasting time on celebrations and get back to work cleaning the aircraft.

Onboard the transport, Rob and most of the team played another cutthroat game of cards. Afterward, they settled down for a few more hours of sleep. Not Moralez though, he was unusually quiet and sat out during the game, just not in the mood to play because his thoughts were on his sister, Rita. He sat listening to the endless drone of the engines and wondered if he would ever see her again. Finally, his mind gave in to his weary body's demands, and he drifted off.

When the transport moved over the coast, it hit some rough air. The pilot did his best to steady the transport, but it continued to jerk up and down in the turbulence.

Stirred by the violent vibrations of the plane, Rob awoke from a deep sleep. He ambled to his feet but was almost knocked off them as he headed to the cockpit. In an instant, the rest of the team was wide awake, all of them wide-eyed and wondering what the hell was going on. The transport kept rocking for a few more minutes, then finally began to settle down.

"What the hell?" Tex said, rubbing his eyes and feeling the uneasiness in his stomach as the plane began to descend.

Rob came back a few moments later with word from the pilots. "Won't be long now, boys. Cap'n says maybe another ten or fifteen minutes."

Everyone was eager to get down on the ground again so they could get moving toward the final leg of their journey. It had been a long flight and it had already taken its toll.

Just as Tex stood to stretch his legs, red lights began to flash, indicating that it was time to buckle in for landing. "Damn it," he cursed as he toppled back into his seat.

The transport banked into a wide turn and started to descend. The big plane came in slow, with its nose up, and floated over the runway, then touched down for a surprisingly smooth landing that had everyone onboard breaking out in cheers. The time for payback was getting closer, and some of them were almost salivating as they thought about it.

"General," Agent Foster said, "I've got more pictures for you, courtesy of Cy-Com. Copies are on the way to you as we speak, and the president has the data. He called for an emergency cabinet meeting this morning."

"Sounds serious. What's going on?" The general asked with a start.

"We're not sure, but there's lots of activity at the target area." Foster replied. "Looks like some type of tanker trucks coming and going."

"Tankers? What kind are we talking about?"

"Could be fuel trucks of some kind," Foster elaborated. "General, my gut tells me they could be prepping another plane, but I don't wanna believe it."

Smithfield checked his watch. "Hmm. I was under the impression the monsters have missiles, but maybe you're right. Maybe they're fueling up another bird, another oversized kamikaze. We can't let that happen again, Agent Foster," he sighed. "I don't like this at all. Our team is eight to ten hours from their intended target. Let's just pray they make it their in time. The president may have to give the order to take it out, regardless of the objections of the secretary of state and others. We might lose a few Iraqi citizens in the crossfire, but at this point, we might have to settle for collateral damage, harsh as that sounds."

"I understand, General, and I have to agree with you," Foster said. "Desperate times, I suppose."

"Very desperate, I'm afraid," he said before he hung up the phone.

As soon as he disconnected with Agent Foster, Smithfield put in a call to his contact in Saudi Arabia. "I wanna know the minute that transport arrives at the airfield," he said, in no uncertain terms.

Meanwhile, in the White House, the president gave the orders. The U.S. Air Force was placed on high alert. Special high-altitude, radar-scanning aircraft and F-16 fighter jets were placed on continuous patrols along the U.S. East Coast. The wheels were set in motion, and an attack on the terrorists in Afghanistan was about to become a reality.

Rob and his team unloaded their gear and departed from the transport. Light Force moved off the tarmac, toward the sprawling Saudi airbase. The first thing they noticed was the dry, searing heat and the desert landscape in the distance. A tall officer and his staff greeted them at the gate. The team stood at attention and saluted.

"Welcome, gentlemen," the officer said, looking the team over. "I'm Captain Willems, we have been expecting you."

Handshakes were shared before Light Force was escorted across the airfield and into the massive headquarters building.

The captain continued, "My assistant will show you to your quarters. Surely you are exhausted after such a long flight. Unfortunately, we don't have much time for R&R, as darkness will fall in about four hours." He smiled at Rob and handed an envelope to him. "You may want to look this over. Also, there will be a briefing before takeoff."

The team was escorted downstairs, and everyone was surprised at the size of the room and the furnishings. There was a phone, as well as a small kitchen, stocked with plenty of food.

As soon as Moralez stowed his gear, he grabbed the phone and made a long-distance call to his parents in New Jersey.

"Hello? Moralez residence."

"Hey, Pop," Moralez said, thrilled to hear his father's voice. "It's Jimmy. How is everything?"

"Jim!? Where are you, son? I've been trying to reach you."

"You know I can't tell you that, Pop," Moralez replied. "This is the first chance I've had to call. Have you heard from Rita? How is she?"

Moralez could tell something was wrong when he sensed hesitation in his father's voice. "We, uh… Son, I'm afraid we don't know what's happened to her," the man said, clearly shaken. "We've made several calls to the police, and your mother has spoken with many of your sister's friends. I even went to the police station yesterday. Everything is in such shambles that it took an hour before I could even talk with someone."

"And what did they say, Dad?" Moralez asked, more worried than he was before.

"The PD assured me they'll let us know the minute they find her. We do know she was at work in the city on 9/11. The police are looking for lots of people, as you might imagine."

It took a moment for Moralez to compose himself and reply, "I can't do anything for her right now but pray. Pop. I'm sure they'll find her alive and well."

Father and son continued to talk, trying to reassure each other that Rita was okay. When Moralez hung up, though, he wondered if he would ever see his sister again.

Rob and the others could see how upset Moralez was, burning with anger that rivaled their own, and they gathered around their comrade in distress and tried to be of some comfort to him.

Tears ran down Moralez's face as he stood and cried, "My Rita! First chance I get, I'm gonna kill all those terrorist bastards!"

Rob pulled Moralez aside. "Listen, man, I know you're angry. Hell, we're all itchin' for a shot at them, but we have to maintain the mission objective, at all costs."

"Yeah, yeah," Moralez snapped, jerking his arm away from Rob and turning to sit down so he could pray for his sister. .

Damn it, Rob thought to himself. *I'm gonna have to keep a close eye on that one, or he might get outta control and compromise the entire mission.*

The parts for the big jet finally arrived, and they were carefully unloaded from the truck and set on the work platform, next to the damaged engine. Amwa Binfudi glared at the mechanics, angry that it was taking so long. Under their leader's scornful watch, the repairmen began the long, tedious process of replacing the main turbine bearings on the massive engine. Once again, the clock was ticking, carrying them ever closer to the moment of takeoff.

Chapter 10

Into the Breach

Back at the airbase, Rob and his team were up from a few hours of much-needed sleep. They gathered at the table and enjoyed a good meal. As they ate, Rob couldn't help but notice that Moralez was very quiet.

Before long, their escort arrived, and they were on their way. They were led into a huge hangar, where they were greeted by Captain Willems and his flight crew. Rob and his men stared in amazement at the bizarre-looking aircraft parked in the hangar. It resembled a flying saucer, with its flat, low-angled front and sides, but it was, in fact, the high-tech B-1 stealth bomber.

Captain Willems introduced his flight crew to the team, and handshakes were given all around as he moved up onto the boarding platform and called everyone to attention. He smiled as he looked over his troops and commenced with his speech. "Now is the time for action! This mission is of the highest priority, so much so that the president himself called a few minutes ago, with a few words to pass on to you. He wishes you all Godspeed and success, and he said he will be praying for your safe return."

Encouraged by his message, the troops dispersed and began boarding the massive, black, triangular aircraft. The flight leader's tag was Slick, and he quickly walked over and shook hands with Rob. "Well, Lieutenant, what do ya think of her?" He asked with a smile and a nod toward the plane.

Rob looked at the bomber and asked, "A pretty, cool piece of technology, if you ask me, but looks aren't everything. How's she fly?"

Slick smiled proudly, as if he'd invented the bomber himself. "Like a dream, almost by herself most of the time."

For the next few minutes, Slick and his crew gave Rob and his men a quick tour of the aircraft. They went over the details of the custom-made setup for their jump. In short, each man would leap out through the bomb bay doors, one after the other, in quick succession.

Once their gear was aboard, everyone settled back in their seats. The jet engines whirred to life, and the bomber slowly crept out of the hangar.

Inside the stealth bomber, Rob sat next to Moralez as he addressed the team. "Finally, we're underway. We all need to remember the importance of this mission. It is our time to make our mark, to pay back these people for what they did to our country. Still, as angry as we all are, we need to keep our heads straight on this one, people. There is no room for mistakes, and we're all in this together. No man left behind!"

The group broke out in cheers, and Moralez raised his clenched fist in the air. "It's payback time, boys. Let's go kick some serious terrorist butt."

"Light Force! Light Force!" Tex chanted, riling the team up even more.

Rob could feel the intensity and the go-get-'em spirit of his men. He sat back with a smile on his face, satisfied and knowing he had accomplished readying his very capable team for the fight to come.

Out on the tarmac, Captain Willems and his staff watched as the B-1 made its final turn and squared up on the runway. The pilot throttled up, and the sleek aircraft zipped down the runway and lifted off at a steep, rocket-like climb, slamming the men back in their seats from the G-forces. Straightaway, Rob noticed something different about the stealth flight. There was no vibration and not much engine noise at all, just the feeling of incredible acceleration.

The pilot eased back on the throttle and started to level off as the bomber reached cruising altitude. The co-pilot loaded the final coordinates into the flight computer. The high-tech bomber was now in full stealth mode. Undetectable to radar, the flying shadow would glide over Iraqi airspace, and no one on the ground would have any idea they were there.

As the plane flew on, Rob couldn't stop thinking about Ashley. He missed her already, especially her smile. He prayed that he would see her again, that he would feel her warm embrace. *Life's too short,* he thought, finally making up his mind. *I love her, and I have to go through with it. I know she's the one for me, so there's no point in waiting.* He wasn't sure if she would accept his proposal or not, but as soon as he got back home, he would buy her a nice ring, take her to their favorite place, and ask for her hand in marriage.

At Central Command, General Smithfield was relieved when the call came through, the one he'd been so anxiously waiting for.

"Light Force is airborne," Captain Willems informed him, "They are on their way to the target."

Smithfield was glad to hear it, and as soon as he hung up, he immediately punched in the number of Defense Secretary Moreland's secure line.

Moreland was heading for the door, on his way to the morning cabinet meeting, when his phone rang. He was glad to hear from Smithfield, particularly since he was calling to let him know the ball was rolling. He thanked Smithfield for the heads-up and talked with him for a few minutes before hanging up, grabbing his briefcase, and heading out to yet another marathon meeting. The plan for a massive strike on the Taliban in Afghanistan was in its final phases, and there couldn't have been better news than that in the wake of such a disaster.

In New York City, the slow, painful process of cleaning up the gigantic tangle of twisted steel beams and debris, once the majestic and iconic Twin Towers, continued. The chances of finding any additional survivors had significantly diminished. Every day, more determined rescue personnel arrived or returned, many with search dogs to accompany them. They left the site exhausted and covered in dust and grime, but each gave it their all, without one utterance of complaint.

Ashley soon returned from her condo after spending some time in the city with her parents. She was relieved that they were okay, but a deep sorrow lingered in her heart for the victims and their families. She had to head back to work in a few days, at a temporary location. Chase had a crew working around the clock to begin operations again; the world simply couldn't remain frozen forever.

Ashley was worried about Rob and thought of him often. She'd never really worried about his missions before, but for some reason, she had a bad feeling about this one. She missed him severely and prayed that she would see his handsome, smiling face again.

Out at sea, military forces prepared as they moved toward the Persian Gulf. In coordination with British Air and Naval forces, the U.S. Navy Fifth Fleet navigated the Arabian Sea, full speed ahead. U.S. and British submarines, armed with Tomahawk cruise missiles approached the coast of Pakistan. On land, at remote airbases in the Middle East, preparations were underway for a massive air strike against the Taliban in Afghanistan. High-tech B-1-B and B-2 bombers, along with a variety of equally impressive aircraft, were on high alert. The international plan to flush out Osami Bind Leden and the evil terrorists who were defending him was about to come to fruition.

Back in Washington, the president and his staff were working on a list of non-negotiable demands to submit to Taliban leaders. The American people demanded justice, and U.S. Senate and House leaders came forward to offer their full support to the president, as did the European Union. Russia issued a statement, declaring that they would stand on the side of justice. America was definitely not alone in the fight, for a great portion of the world at large was on her side.

In Iraq, radar screens might have picked up a slight flicker as the sleek stealth bomber soared over their airspace. Aboard that bomber, the team was readying themselves for their high-altitude jump. Each man was fitted with a special suit designed to protect them from the thin, freezing air at 10,000 feet. The suits also enabled a limited amount of navigation during freefall.

Each was also equipped with a night-vision headset. Word soon came that the aircraft was closing in on the target area, and a red light flashed above the cockpit doors. The team formed a line, with Rob at the lead.

Rob looked out at the night sky and yelled over his shoulder, "Remember to move into formation once we clear the aircraft. Follow my lead to the target!"

Tex smiled as he put his helmet on. "We're as ready as we can be. God help us all!"

The light changed from red to green, and the huge bay doors slowly swung open. Rob was the first out, with the rest plummeting behind him in quick succession. Once they were clear of the aircraft, the team gradually began to move into a V formation. Rob could feel his senses heightening as the excitement and weightlessness of freefall came over him. Down they streaked, through the clouds and toward their intended target on hostile, foreign soil.

At a predetermined altitude, Rob's GPS unit began flashing. He gave the signal to his comrades and pulled his cord. His chute blew open, and for just a moment, he felt a strong pull as he was flung upward from the power of the expanding parachute.

The team began to slowly drift toward the target below them. Tex was the first to touch down in the reddish-brown sand of the open desert. He could feel the coolness of the night as he watched the rest of the team drop and roll in around him. Quickly, the team gathered their chutes and buried their jump gear. Josh made his way over to Rob, and they checked the uplink communications and were glad to see the display was working, with the green indicator lights flashing on the screen to reveal their target.

Tex gathered around Rob with the others and wiped the sand from his eyes. "Sir, everyone is ready to roll."

Rob pointed toward the mountains jutting out of the horizon. "Weapons hot! Let's move out."

Quickly, the team moved out single file, into the seemingly endless sand and rock of the desert terrain.

Once the bomber was clear of Iraqi airspace, they radioed back to base, "The package has been delivered."

Captain Willems was relieved to get the news, and he immediately picked up his phone and called General Smithfield at Central Command. It was only a matter of moments before the news made it to the top of the grapevine. Smithfield was relieved; Light Force was on the ground in Iraq, and they were moving at a fast clip toward their destination.

About ten miles north of the drop zone, a group of terrorists drove along in an old Jeep truck, making their way toward the open desert. In the moonlit night, their leader, Mosowi Ari, caught just a glimpse of something dropping in the distant horizon, a blip in the sky. He was unsure of what it was, but was certainly eager to find out.

Unaware of the impending danger, Light Force pushed on toward their target. They kept up a brisk pace as they covered the miles of brown sand and rock.

Rob signaled for them to halt when he sensed a change in the terrain up ahead. They had come to the beginning of a rocky descent that led to the valley below. Rob took off his helmet and wiped his sweaty face. The sun was just beginning to lighten the horizon, but before long, he knew it would be getting kicking hot. The team gathered around and took a break for some much-needed water. They had just covered about a four-mile run, each man hauling forty pounds of gear on his sweaty back.

Tex took a long pull from his canteen and grinned from ear to ear when Rob poured some water over his head. "Hot damn, that was a good run. I got a feelin' it's gonna be like an oven out here by afternoon though."

"You got that right, man," Rob replied as he scanned the valley below. He pointed and continued, "Listen up! Check out that small clump of trees way down there."

Everyone took a good look with their field glasses.

"How far you think that is, sir?" Moralez asked.

Rob checked his navigation uplink. "Looks to be about another six miles, and it just so happens to be in line with where we need to be. Let's rest a few minutes, then get to that cover by at least 013:00 to get the hell outta this sun."

Josh, their field medic, added, "Take your salt pills and watch your water. We need to make it last."

With that said, the team slowly began picking their way down the rocky ridgeline.

Back at the terrorist base, the final preparations for the jet engine repair were underway. The mechanics had been working through the night, so the new bearings were in place, and the reassembly was almost complete. The leader, Amwa Binfudi, was already up and anxiously waiting for the aircraft to be airborne and on its way to deliver a devastating blow to the innocent people of America, all in the name of their so called jihad (holy war). By any stretch of any sane person's imagination, there was nothing holy about it.

Nevertheless, the clock was ticking once again, moving ever closer to the moment of takeoff.

Back in Washington, the president finished his briefing with his military advisors. The morning cabinet meeting would cover the progress of the plan to strike down the evil and bring some justice to the American people. The president was happy to hear that everything was falling into place, that the fist of war was about to strike a mighty blow. If the terrorists only knew a fraction of what was coming their way, they would have been running for their lives.

As the war progressed, many would hide like cowards among the innocent civilians, too afraid to come out and fight unless they could catch their enemies in an ambush. That was how they worked, planting bombs, even blowing themselves up, or making a hit and scurrying away. The American military quickly adapted to their urban guerrilla warfare, though, and before long, they were able to dig them out like exterminators rooting bugs out of the cracks and crevices. Unfortunately, all that digging came with a price, at the cost of American lives. The warriors fought on, though, hoping to destroy the terrorists before they could gain a foothold.

Chapter 11

The Desert

In the remote desert mountains of Iraq, Rob and his team were about halfway to the clump of trees. The searing heat was intense, almost flesh-melting, as they stopped to take some water.

Out of breath and sweat soaked, Tex wiped his face with his bandana. "Hey, man, tell me again why I wanted to come on this dumbass mission."

Rob smiled. "Because you like me so much that you'll follow me anywhere, even to a shithole like this!"

Tex busted out laughing, and the rest of the team joined in. It was good to laugh, as it helped ease the tension.

Rob stood before his men. "I know it sucks out here, fellas, but we've gotta keep moving before someone spots us in the open valley."

The team agreed and quickly got into formation to make the final run to the shady spot in the distance. As if the torturous heat was not bad enough to contend with, the wind was picking up, swirling mini-sandstorms in the air around them. Every exposed area of their skin was pelted with what felt like bee stings as the grains tore into them with the force of the drafts, and the sand that crept into their nostrils and mouths made it difficult to breathe. The team stopped just long enough to put on their facemasks, and then continued on.

Only about five miles from Rob and his team, Mosowi and his band of terrorists were busy searching for any signs of activity. So far, they'd found nothing, but Mosowi trusted his instincts, and he knew he had seen something; he was certain something was amiss in his desert. They had no idea that they were so close to the Light Force landing zone (LZ), as they had not yet picked up their trail. They continued on in the general direction of the team, with evil intent on their minds.

The American people were finally over the shock of what had happened in New York City, and the initial shock and awe were beginning to morph into even stronger feelings of anger, resolve, and enhanced patriotism. A swell of American pride was rising among the people, as evidenced by the fact that military recruiting offices were jam-packed with volunteers who wanted a chance to serve and get involved in the fight, brave souls who were ready to take revenge on the terrorists who had so callously infiltrated their homeland.

In New York City, workers of all trades were in the process of getting things running again. Ashley was back to work for the first time in weeks, and that did help—at least to some degree—to take her mind off of her constant worries about Rob. She missed him to a heart-aching level and prayed every night for his safe return, but in the meantime, she had to be a functioning member of society again.

Rob and his team were ecstatic when they finally finished their desperate dash for cover. Soaked in sweat, with their uniforms covered in sand, they were on the verge of heat exhaustion, and the coolness of the shade was a welcome relief. In spite of the medic's warning to mind their water rations carefully, Rob and Josh stripped of their shirts and doused themselves with water, and it didn't take long for the rest of the team to join in.

After a few moments of cooldown time, Rob smiled as he looked at his comrades. "That was a helluva run, boys!" He took a pull from his canteen, gulping heavily. "Now that we're in the shade, we can get some real R&R and stay put till sunset."

Rob checked the uplink, and their coordinates revealed that they were about three miles east of their intended target. He then instructed his team to set up a temporary shelter. Some of the men began to hollow out the ground below the trees, and the rest spread out to gather small branches and pieces of wood. The idea was to create some protection from the wind that was slowly starting to increase, tossing more sand their way. It didn't take them long to put the finishing touches on their little hideout, and it was a nice, undercover place to eat and rest for the adventures of the coming night.

At the terrorist base, workers had to stop what they were doing and cover the jet engines to protect them from the sandstorm. Amwa Binfudi was furious, running around and shouting orders left and right. The aircraft was in the final stage of repairs and was on standby for takeoff within the hour, but now they had to wait out a storm. Once again, their hideous plan had to take a back burner, this time to Mother Nature, and Binfudi was none too happy about it. He wanted to change history forever, and he was growing weary of the distractions that kept him from doing so.

At the Cy-Com Center, Stan Gustan was tracking the uplink signal. He picked up the phone and called Agent Foster. "Looks like the team landed on target and have moved about three miles toward their objective," he announced. "They seem to be holding at their current location."

The agent was happy to hear the news that the team was on the ground and in place. She thanked him and dialed General Smithfield. Within minutes, the good news was falling on the ears of the American president.

Back in the desert, Mosowi and his men had finally picked up the Light Force trail, when they spotted some footprints near the landing zone. Based on the depth of the imprints, Mosowi assumed they were dealing with a small group, carrying heavy weapons. They followed the tracks as far as they could, until the dust-filled wind picked up to a point that drove them all back to the cover of their Jeep. They now knew what general direction they should go, but Mosowi worried the tracks would be lost, covered in sand within a very short time.

Meanwhile, not too far away, Rob and his team had finished their MREs and were huddled under their makeshift cover, with their facemasks on. The winds and blowing sand howled outside, but they were pretty cozy in their self-built little shack.

"'Nighty night, y'all," Tex said, using his backpack for a pillow and his poncho for a cover as he stretched out on the ground to catch a few winks. "Don't let the bedbugs bite!"

"Can you keep watch for the first couple hours?" Rob asked Josh.

"Sure," Josh said. "I'm on it." Visibility was very poor as Josh scanned the perimeter. He'd never seen anything like it, and he was sure no one was going to be able to traverse through it, not even the terrorists who were used to living in the hostile conditions.

Rob leaned back against the dirt wall of the ditch and tried to catch a nap. It took him a while to unwind, but he finally drifted off, thinking of Ashley and her smiling face.

At the Cy-Com Surveillance Center, Agent Foster sat with Stan Gustan, sipping her coffee as she carefully watched the satellite display. "I wonder why they're not moving?" she said.

Stan took a sip from his own mug, then answered, "Who knows? Maybe they ran into some trouble or are hiding from something. I'm sure it's nothing, or we woulda heard about it."

Foster smiled. "You're probably right. If they were compromised, the team would have tried to contact us." Suddenly, something struck her. "Hey, let's do a check on the weather at their location."

Stan flipped a few switches, and within seconds, they had their answer. "By George, you're right, Foster. Looks like they're holed up at the tail end of a monster windstorm."

Foster smiled again and turned to Gustan. "How long do you think it will last?"

"There's no telling for sure, but…" Stan paused and used the weather computer to complete a few quick calculations and estimates. "Looks like they should be clear in about an hour or two."

"Good," Foster replied as she stood. "I'm going to my office to make a few calls. Let me know the minute they start moving again."

Back in her office, Agent Foster ordered some lunch and made a call to General Smithfield. She advised the general of the situation in Iraq and assured him that they were watching it closely. Smithfield agreed with their conclusion and asked her to let him know as soon as the team was moving again.

In New York City, the seemingly endless task of removing debris at ground zero continued. City hospitals were finally beginning to catch their breath after an onslaught of patients who required 'round-the-clock care.

One Hispanic female, a World Trade Center victim, had been brought to the ICU at City Hospital. The hardworking doctors had seen little improvement and were beginning to think she might not make it out of the coma she'd been in since her arrival, but everything was still touch and go for her and many others. The hospital staff and the police had tried to find some way to identify her, but so far, nothing had turned up. Not knowing who she was or anything about her medical history only made her condition all the more precarious, and as of yet, no loved ones had shown up to ask about her.

Chapter 12

Silent Strike

In Washington, the president and his cabinet had received news that U.S. and British Air and Naval forces were in their final position for launch. They also just received word that the vote from a closed session of Congress was unanimous, in favor of a military response against the terrorists.

After conferring with his secretary of state and defense, the president gave the final go-ahead for the massive attack to get underway; it was no easy feat to push the proverbial button, but the president knew something had to be done to stop the terrorist virus that was infecting far too many nations, his own included. The terrorists were blatant in their attacks, as if they thought they were invincible, and he intended to use military might to prove them wrong about that.

The sandstorm finally gave its last hoorah in Iraq, and Rob quickly moved to gather up his gear and get his men in order and on the move again. "Time to move out, gentlemen! The good weather won't last long, and once that breeze stops, it's gonna get boiling hot real quick. Tex and I will take point. Josh, you and Moralez watch our backs. Stay sharp, people! Now form up and move out single file, weapons hot."

The team then headed out for their final run to the target location. After an hour of hard running in the punishing heat, the team reached the top of a vast mountain ridge. They stopped to rest, have a drink, and check their coordinates.

Rob scanned the area below and spotted the outline of something in the distant valley floor. His gut told him they had reached the target. One last uplink confirmed his suspicion that their target was at hand. Quickly, Rob and his comrades descended. They took cover in a dried-out riverbed and snaked toward the end of the valley in the distance.

A large display screen lit up in the Cy-Com Center, with a small, blue light blinking in the middle of it. Gustan checked the coordinates and was relieved to find that the signal was coming from the Light Force GPS, now moving quickly toward the target.

Agent Foster was just about to leave her office at the Cy-Com Center when her phone started ringing. She picked up and was thrilled to hear the news. She hurried down the elevator and entered the surveillance center.

Gustan, obviously happy to see her, offered her some coffee before they sat down to look at the display screen together.

Foster confirmed that the team was approaching the target and anxiously waited for the uplink line to start ringing. She almost couldn't believe her eyes as she watched the blue blip stop blinking just before the monitor went blank. "What the...?" she asked, looking at Gustan in horror. "What the hell just happened?"

Gustan frantically checked his computer and the uplink from the Cy-Com satellite. "I-I don't know," he admitted. "Everything looks good on our end."

"We need to know what's going on, Gustan. I don't like this one bit," Agent Foster said.

"I don't like it either. We just somehow lost their signal, like they turned it off or something. But why would they?"

Speechless and clueless, the two just stared at the display in disbelief, hoping and praying that Light Force would come back online.

Light Force was moving ever closer to their target, but Rob gave the hold signal as they came to the end of the ravine they'd just run through. The team knowingly spread out in a defensive position.

Rob quickly and quietly located their high-powered field glasses and ambled to the top of the ravine with Tex in tow. He couldn't believe his eyes as he focused on the giant airliner. He could feel his adrenaline pumping as he located a dozen or more figures running around the rear of the aircraft, moving what appeared to be sheets of plastic. "Jesus!" he said, turning to Tex and staring at him with wide eyes. "It's a jumbo jet!"

"What the hell?" Tex replied. "How the fuck did they get another plane?"

Rob handed Tex the glasses. "Take a look for yourself. I don't know how they got their hands on it, but they're sure as hell getting that thing ready for takeoff." Rob turned to Josh and yelled over his shoulder, "Calculate the coordinates and call in the airstrike immediately!"

Josh nodded, took out his range finder, and quickly punched in the coordinates. He unhooked the uplink from his backpack, flipped the send switch, turned on the headset, and called into Cy-Com to give them the green light for the attack, but there was clearly something wrong with his equipment. He gave it a firm smack a couple times, but that did little to remedy the problem. "Rob, I've got trouble. The uplink's not workin' for some reason!"

Rob's hands began to tremble as he thought about what could happen if that plane managed to get airborne. He replied, "Keep trying! We need to make that call!"

Tex handed Rob the field glasses. "Looks like we got a big problem, my friend. They get that bird in the air, and a lotta innocent people are gonna go down."

Rob took another look at the aircraft and the runway that extended out into the valley floor. He turned to Josh again. "You got that uplink working yet, buddy?"

"No, sir," Josh replied. "I don't know what the hell's wrong with it, but we're getting nothing. The battery's fine, but it seems like the signal's getting blocked somehow," he reasoned, having no idea that they were currently situated in an area of significant underground ore deposits that formed a magnetic shield around them, virtually creating a firewall for their uplink signal.

Rob tried to calm down as he pondered their options. *That plane can't take off. It's up to us now. We have to do it.* As soon as the first feasible idea came to him, he quickly gathered his team. "Listen up! Whatever happens, boys, we can*not* let that bird off the ground!" he yelled, pointing at the aircraft.

"Get me in a good enough spot, and I can shoot the tires," Tex offered. "Even a plane won't get far on a flat."

Rob smiled at his friend. "Thanks for the offer, Tex, but I don't wanna take any chances on this one. We're gonna have to do more damage than that and take this baby out ourselves. Whatever we're doing, we'd better do it quick. My gut tells me they plan to take off within the hour, now that the weather's cooperating."

"Yeah, well, so much for that bullshit of time bein' on our side," Tex said, "but it sure does fly when you *ain't* havin' fun!"

"Right," Rob said, shaking his head. "Look, Tex, you and Moralez get into some desert camo and sneak out to the middle section of the runway. You guys set up our claymores and a tripwire across it."

"And the big plane goes boom? I like it!" Tex replied, wearing a grin as big as the state he was named after.

"Me too! Let's blow those suckers all over the desert," Moralez replied with a smile.

Rob continued, "Phil, you and I will stay tight and cover them until the claymores are in place. Josh, you and Adams head back up the ridge and dig us in for a defensive location. The rest of us will meet you there once the deed is done."

"Yes, sir!" everyone said, then quickly broke off to do as they'd been ordered.

Unaware of what was taking place out on the runway, Binfudi and his terrorists scrambled around, doing their final checks to make sure all the repairs were finished. The aircraft was cleaned up, and the pilots were in place for takeoff as soon as the pre-flight checks were accomplished.

Binfudi prayed to his so-called God that all their hard work would pay off, with a final, devastating blow to America. The waiting and anticipation for the moment of takeoff was wearing on the terrorist leader as he paced around the aircraft, barking out hasty final orders to his men.

Their plan was to disassemble and remove all remnants of the operation immediately following the lift off of the aircraft. They would be on their way back home to Afghanistan by the end of the day, or so they hoped.

Further away, Mosowi and his men were on the move again, as the raw power of the desert sun was beating down on them. Mosowi was sure the enemy was at hand, so, like a pack of hungry wolves on the hunt, they relentlessly pressed on, searching for their prey, heading in the general direction of the tracks they'd seen before the storm set in. When they arrived at the base of a rocky mountain ridge, Mosowi gave the order to abandon the Jeep and continue on foot. The going was tough in the rock-strewn, sandy terrain, but not one of his men dared to complain.

At the lookout point, Rob nervously watched as Tex and Moralez crawled back from the runway, having done their dirty deed. With the claymores in place, they all started moving back up the ridgeline as quickly as possible. Just as the four of them reached the top of the ridge, the unmistakable sounds of the huge jet engines filled the air. Josh signaled them over to their hideout, and the rest of the team piled in and took cover.

Binfudi and his terrorists were full of excitement as the jumbo jet slowly crept onto the runway. The sun was well over the huge mountaintops in the distant horizon. The pilot squared up to the runway. The plane lurched forward as the pilot released the brakes and went full throttle. Binfudi and his terrorists jumped for joy and fired their weapons in the air in celebration as the plane accelerated, while Rob and his Light Force team held their breath and crossed their fingers in their defensive bunker only a short distance away.

The nose of the aircraft lifted just in time to miss the tripwire, but the rear wheels plowed into it. Suddenly, there was a bright flash of light, followed by a ground-shaking explosion directly under the back of the aircraft just before it went airborne. The pilots desperately struggled to gain control as the shockwave from the blast rocked the vessel almost bringing it down.

Binfudi and his men stopped their dancing and clapping and just looked on in shock, trying to comprehend the brevity of what was happening. They were relieved to see that the aircraft gained control, and was still climbing up into the mountain air. Where did the explosion come from? Clearly, someone had infiltrated their supposedly secret operation in the secluded desert, which wouldn't bode well for any of them.

The pilot nervously checked his settings and leaned on the throttle to gain altitude. Little did he or the flight crew know that a hot piece of steel shrapnel had inflicted a slow but fatal leak in the hydraulic flight control system.

Rob and the team watched in shock and disbelief as the pilot somehow managed to regain control after the violent blast; instead of crashing, the jumbo jet started to increased altitude and, before long, disappeared over the jagged mountain peaks.

After taking a moment to gather his thoughts, Rob turned to Josh. "Check that uplink again. We have to let our people know what is heading their way!"

"Yes sir!" Josh replied, nervously pressing and turning the uplink controls to make the urgent call to Cy-Com. As he worked the computer uplink controls, and called into

Cy-Com. Rob could tell it was bad news from the look of bewilderment on Josh's face. He gathered his team up close again and pointed at the distant ridgeline. "We need to haul ass over there, double-time. They'll be coming for us now. We have to get out of here. Plus, the extra height, and jagged edge of the ridge will give us a clearer line of fire when they come up the trail."

"Yes, sir!" the team members replied, everyone moved out with all the speed and precision of a band of mountain lions, up over the uneven, rocky terrain they scrambled.

Chapter 13

Fight

At the airstrip, Binfudi was in a full-blown rage as he called his men before him. "Someone is among us!" He pointed out into the valley. "I want those infidels, dead or alive! Find them! Go! Go now!" he screamed.

His men ran around in a panic, grabbing their weapons and gear. A large group of them jumped in the back of their truck and headed down the runway. Another group went up toward the ridgeline on foot.

In the distance, Mosowi and his group had heard the explosion and were heading in that direction at full speed. The noose was beginning to tighten around Rob and his team.

At Central Command, General Smithfield was in his office when a call came through from Agent Foster. "Smithfield here," he said.

"General, the uplink is still down," she reported grimly, "but they do have a GPS link working, so we can see that the team is at least up and moving again."

Smithfield was relieved to have any news at all, and it was a good sign that Light Force was no longer stagnant or trapped. "Call me the minute that uplink's back online," he told Foster, then hung up the phone. The general had a bad feeling in the pit of his stomach, that niggling fear that something bad was about to happen. He only hoped that misfortune would fall on their enemies and not on Rob and his team.

The terrorists on the aircraft were happy to be on their way. The pilots were busy punching in the coordinates on the flight computer. The aircraft was twenty-five miles out from the base already, and with a good tailwind, they estimated they would be at the southeastern coast of America in eight hours. A more experienced crew would have checked the little gauge at the bottom right of the cockpit display and noticed that their hydraulic fluid was moving down toward a dangerously low level. It was just a matter of time before they began to lose control of the flying bomb.

At City Hospital, Mr. Moralez and his family were gathered in the waiting room, praying. After a long, tireless search they had finally found Rita, but she was only barely clinging to life. All they could do was trust the doctors and pray to God. Desperately, they hung on to their hope that she would soon wake up.

Suddenly, one of the doctors burst through the waiting room doors, wearing a smile on his face. Mr. Moralez was the first to notice, and he stood to greet the doctor who was quickly approaching them.

"She is beginning to come out of the coma," the doctor proudly announced, shaking Mr. Moralez's hand.

The family laughed, cried, and clapped their hands, elated by the news and begging to see her.

"We have upgraded her condition to critical, but she is still very weak," the doctor said. "We will know more tomorrow, but for now, visits must be extremely brief. She needs her rest."

Mr. and Mrs. Moralez hurried in to see their daughter. The first thing they noticed was that the cobweb of countless tubes and many of the beeping, buzzing machines were gone. Rita was sitting more upright, with her eyes partially open. As they moved closer to the bed, she slowly extended her hand, and the tears of joy began to flow.

After reaching the crest of the treacherous ridgeline, Light Force jumped on what appeared to be an old trail.

Rob was on point, with Tex close behind him, but he stopped abruptly and gave the hold signal to his team. "Let's take a little break, boys. I wanna take a look back and see who's following us." He turned to Josh. "Keep trying that uplink. We've gotta get the word out."

"Yes, sir," Josh said, just as frustrated with the equipment as Rob was. "I know something's blocking our signal, but for the life of me, I can't figure out what."

"All you can do is try your best," Tex assured him, giving him a pat on the back. "Sometimes I think we were all better off before all these new-fangled gadgets anyway, but I'd sure as hell like to hear that this one's back online."

Rob and Tex moved back to the edge of the rocky ridgeline and saw a dust cloud forming in the valley below. "Looks like we got some company coming," Rob said.

Tex nodded. "Roger on that, sir. I'm guessin' that a possible band of bad guys are about twenty minutes away."

Rob picked up his rifle. "We'd better get the team moving again."

As soon as Rob gave the order to move out, Josh grabbed his arm and handed him the headset. "It just started working, sir!"

"Good work!" Rob replied as he scrambled to get the headset on. "Cen-Com, this is Light Force. Cen-Com, do you copy?"

Stan Gustan almost fell off his chair as he scrambled to pick up his headset when he heard Rob's voice. "This is Cen-Com. Go ahead, Light Force! Copy?"

Gustan could not believe his ears as Rob filled him in on what had happened.

"We're ready for extraction, as soon as we have an LZ secured," Rob said.

"You got it," Gustan said. "I'll pass the message on."

With the call for help finished, Rob turned to his men again. "Let's move out, double-time! Tex, you take point for now." He pointed up the old trail. "We need to secure an LZ. Help is on the way, gentlemen!"

Gustan picked up the hotline and called Agent Foster. Stunned, she quickly hung up and made a call. *Oh my God! No! Not another plane,* she thought as she waited for the call to connect, just a few seconds that seemed to stretch into an eternity of agony.

General Smithfield picked up the phone in a bit of a huff, tired of being interrupted. "Smithfield here," he grumbled.

"Hello, General. Agent Foster here. The team's uplink is working, and I've got some news from Light Force. They confirmed the target, but were unable to get their uplink working in time to request an airstrike. They tried to take care of the situation themselves but were unsuccessful. General, I'm afraid another airliner is headed our way."

"Another plane?" he boomed into the phone. "Are you telling me those sick terrorist bastards are sending *another* plane over here, Agent Foster?"

"Yes, sir. I'm afraid that's the Intel we've gotten from Light Force. They tried their best to stop it without backup, but they just missed bringing it down with claymores."

Smithfield was at a loss for words a moment as he gathered his thoughts. "How is the team?" he asked. "Are *they* okay?"

"Yes, General. They seem to be all right, but they are on the run, requesting extraction."

Smithfield thanked Foster for the news, hung up with her, and immediately placed a long-distance call to alert the authorities who were waiting on standby at the Saudi Arabian airbase and on a Fifth Fleet aircraft carrier just off the coast. Captain Willems spoke with Smithfield, and it was decided that they would wait for Light Force to call in the exact location of the landing zone. Any calls that came in on the uplink would now be patched straight through to General Smithfield and his staff.

Within a matter of minutes, the commander-in-chief was fully aware of the situation. The president ordered United States military forces to Red Com 4 high-alert status, and the East Coast of America suddenly became the center of the world. All commercial and civilian air traffic was grounded as the sky filled with fighter jets and surveillance aircraft. The new defensive missile systems were online, up and ready to launch, and orders were given to perform continuous sweeps of the U.S. eastern seaboard.

Chapter 14

Destruction

In the skies over northern Iraq, a vibrating jolt rattled the pilots inside the cockpit of the jumbo jet. Warning lights flashed all over the panel. The co-pilot frantically tapped the gauges, and pressed buttons, trying to get an idea on what was wrong with their crippled aircraft.

When the pilot noticed that the plane was losing altitude, he desperately tried to pull up the nose and increased the throttle, but the plane was nonresponsive, since the hydraulic fluid was critically low, too low to build up any pressure. The vessel was little more powerful than a paper airplane at that point, flying with no flaps or rudder controls. Helpless to do anything, the terrorists watched in horror as the craft pitched over on its side and headed toward the ground. As fate would have it, the planes collision was doomed to happen at the original terrorist-controlled training area and airbase it flew out of, a case of what went up having to come down, this time in the form of a quickly plummeting would-be tomb.

Rob and his team were still on the run in the mountains when they detected movement up ahead on the trail. Rob gave a signal to hold tight, and everyone instinctually dropped, with their weapons at the ready.

Mosowi and his band of bad men came into full view, darting their eyes about like wild animals on a scavenger hunt. Slowly, they moved along the trail, weapons ready.

Rob gave the order in a heartbeat, knowing they had to take advantage of the element of surprise while it was still on their side. "Open fire! Fire at will!" he cried.

The terrorists in the front of the column were cut down in a hailstorm of bullets, and Light Force continued spraying the trail with automatic weapons fire. Mosowi was shot in the chest and knocked back off his feet.

One survivor managed to haphazardly fire an RPG before they retreated. The rocket streaked over Rob and landed next to Phil Takis with a thunderous explosion. Phil went down. He was covered with blood, not moving at all.

It took a moment for Rob to recover. His ears were ringing as he tried to gather himself and check on the rest of the team. "Hold your fire! Hold fire!" Rob screamed and signaled.

For a moment, no one moved; the guns fell silent, and the smoke cleared over the trail. Rob ordered his team into defensive positions.

Josh grabbed the medical kit and moved to his fallen comrade. He held Phil still while Tex stripped off his flak jacket and cut his shirt open, drawing loud screams from Phil, who had suffered deep shrapnel wounds in his abdomen. Josh found the morphine and quickly gave Phil a shot. Tex tore some large bandages with his teeth and pressed them against the injuries, applying pressure to help stop the bleeding.

After a few tense moments, the drug took effect, and Phil quieted. Josh checked his wounds and vitals, then looked at Rob and Tex with a shake of his head and a solemn frown on his face, letting them know his grim prognosis.

The rest of the team gathered around as Rob tried his best to comfort their dying brother-in-arms.

Phil didn't speak, but his eyes were as wide as saucers, and blood was spurting from his mouth. Sooner than they all expected, his eyes closed, and his body went limp.

"No pulse…and no breathing," Rob reported softly, letting out a deep sigh.

Josh slowly pulled the blanket up over Phil's face, and all was quiet as the team was flooded with the emotion of losing a good man.

Tex was the first to grab his weapon and scramble to his feet. "Where are those bastards? They're gonna pay for this!"

"Right! Let's go after the freaks!" added Moralez.

Rob wiped the blood from his trembling hands and looked into their angry faces. "Believe me, I want the same thing, but we have to keep our focus if we're gonna make it out of this sandy shithole alive. We owe Phil that, to at least try without losing our heads."

In the airspace over northern Iraq, the terrorists were still frantically trying to gain control of their aircraft. They realized the close vicinity of the airfield and tried to line up with the runway. The flight controllers in the airbase tower could not believe their eyes as the rocking, swaying jumbo jet came into view in the distance. Fire trucks were dispatched, but had they known what was coming their way, that they were on a crash-course with disaster themselves, they would have driven in the opposite direction, as fast as their trucks would take them.

Within a few minutes, the aircraft slammed down hard and careened off the runway, then rammed into the side of a large airplane hangar. For a moment, there was only a loud crunching sound, but that was followed by a super-bright, almost blinding flash of light as the payload began to explode. An orange-red fireball swallowed the entire airbase center and completely destroyed the terrorist training base. The ensuing shockwave, massive, ground-shaking detonation leveled everything within a one-mile radius.

About five miles away, farmers were in their fields, tending to their goats. They felt the ground trembling beneath their feet as the bright flash and rumble of the explosion caught their attention. They watched in amazement as the fireball reached up into the sky. After ten minutes or so, a fine, white, powdery substance began to flurry around them, spreading death and suffering throughout the land.

At the end of the runway, Binfudi and his men scrambled up into the surrounding ridgeline. They had a good lock on the location where the gunfire was coming from, and their vengeful hearts made them determined to find the people responsible for trying to blow up their plane and its precious, deadly cargo. They had no idea of the disaster that was already unfolding from the toxic blast they'd created in their foolishness, that they, themselves, had brought death to their own homeland.

In the distant hills, Rob and what remained of Light Force gathered their gear and finished building a makeshift stretcher. Adams and Moralez hoisted their fallen comrade onto the contraption and followed Rob, Josh, and Tex as they continued along the trail. It was tough going as they worked their way past jagged rocks, potholes and patches of sand.

Just out of sight, three survivors from the firefight were sneaking up on the team. The fanatical terrorists place no value on their own lives; they only lived to bring pain and death to their enemies. They had lost their rifles in the firefight, but they maintained a tight grip on their pistols and knives. Slowly, they sneaked their way closer.

On the ridgeline trail, Rob was determined to find the nearest flat, open area, anything suitable for a safe landing so they could be pulled out. They moved under an outcropping of reddish rock, with Josh covering the flank and Rob on point.

Josh looked back and checked the trail. Everything was quiet for a while, but then he heard some loud, unsettling thumps behind him. When he turned to look again, he couldn't believe his eyes. Three terrorists had jumped on the trail and were drawing their weapons. Josh moved to pull his rifle up, but it was too late; he was clobbered right in the shoulder as the terrorists opened fire, and the force of the hit knocked him right off his feet before he could even cry out a warning.

What happened next only lasted about a minute, but to Rob, it seemed like everything was moving in slow motion. Bullets snapped and popped around him as the team quickly turned and ran back toward Josh.

Of course Tex was the first to get into the action, but as he was running and screaming, a round hit his rifle and knocked it out of his hand. Moralez moved into a prone position, then fired a burst and hit one of the terrorists in the throat; the enemy went down, with a thick spray of crimson spurting from his neck.

Tex pulled his blade as he closed in and jumped right into the fray of remaining terrorists, knocking two of them to the ground with all the force of an NFL linebacker smashing into a Quarterback. He pinned one of them down and slit his throat wide open with his big blade.

The other terrorist started to get up, but he was quickly tackled by Rob, and the two of them hit the ground hard. Locked in a death struggle, Rob knocked the gun out of the terrorist's hand, then put the man in a chokehold and snapped his neck with one quick bone-crunching jerk.

Josh was alive, but on the ground, crying out in pain and writhing like an injured animal. Tex and Moralez moved over to him and tried to settle him down. Moralez grabbed the medical kit and applied a pressure bandage to his wound. Rob held the medic down as Tex injected morphine into his arm. Rob almost instantly felt the tension release from Josh's twitching and damaged shoulder muscles as the powerful drug took effect, relieving his pain and calming him down.

Tex cut off a portion of Josh's shirt and carefully examined his wound. "I ain't no doctor, but it doesn't look too bad. Looks ta me like the bullet went clean through muscle, no bone. We need to clean the sucker and close it up though."

Adams gave Josh some antibiotics and wrapped his shoulder up as tightly as he could.

Josh looked at Tex. "Thanks for the shot. I feel much better."

"Good!" Adams replied as he put his arm in a makeshift sling he fashioned from a few twigs and bandages. "We can't have our doc dying on us!"

Rob smiled as he looked at Josh. "Hang in there, buddy. We're gonna get the hell outta here as soon as we can. Can you walk?"

"I-I think so, as long as we take it easy."

"No problem," Rob replied. "I'll carry your gear."

"Damn, that sure felt good, kicking some terrorist ass," Tex added as he wiped the blood off his hands and his blade. He walked over to the enemy corpses, dragged them to the edge of the ridge, and threw them over.

Rob gave the order to destroy their weapons, and when Josh was ready, the team gathered everything up and continued along the ridgeline trail, carrying their dead comrade and keeping a close eye on their injured and drugged-up medic. Rob stopped now and then to scan the area ahead for any signs of a spot they could use as a landing zone. So far, Josh was holding up fairly well as he walked with his good arm wrapped around Adam's shoulder.

Chapter 15

Good News

In the Command Center, General Smithfield received another call from Agent Foster, and he was glad to hear from her.

"Our intelligence contacts in Iraq, supported by satellite imagery of the area, have indicated that a large airliner crashed. There was a devastating explosion some sixty miles from the target area," she said.

"Hot damn! Maybe them boys got 'em after all."

"Maybe," she said, then went on to fill him in about the reports of a release of toxic chemicals in the ensuing dust cloud.

While Smithfield was relieved to hear that it was highly possible that the rogue aircraft had gone down in flames, he was highly concerned about the biochemical warfare they were using, not to mention that his men were still in Iraq. "We haven't heard anything about a safe extraction point yet," he told Agent Foster. "As soon as we get a pick-up location from Light Force, we'll go in and get our boys outta there."

"I hope that's sooner rather than later, General," she said.

"I agree, Agent Foster." He thanked her for getting him the intelligence and also assured her he would immediately pass the good news up to the president.

Rob and his men took turns carrying the stretcher as they moved along the endless rocky terrain of the mountain trail. So far, Josh seemed to be holding up fairly well. Adams checked his wound and was happy to see that the bleeding had slowed. The team had to move at a slower pace as the terrain changed, with the rocks and boulders increasing in size. After another hour of navigating the trail, Rob and his men stopped to rest and take in some much-needed water.

Tex scanned the surrounding area with his field glasses, then turned to Rob and pointed down the trail. "Looks like a pretty good spot up ahead for the choppers to set down."

Rob took a look through the field glasses and could just make out what looked to be a flat, sandy area off to the side of the trail. "That might do, Tex," he said.

"I hope so. I'm ready to fly this coop," Tex said.

Moralez took a long pull from his canteen and downed another Power Bar, then turned to Rob. "I still can't believe that giant airplane was out in the middle of the desert. What do you think? Was it set to be another terrorist attack on the homeland?"

Tex turned to Moralez. "I'm still wondering why the hell the claymores didn't take it down."

Moralez frowned. "I know. We had those suckers set just right, and the timing was right on."

Rob shook his head as he continued to scan ahead on the trail. "I don't know either, fellas. I was sure the claymores would do the trick. I've got a bad feeling about this whole mess. We need to get the hell outta here! Moralez, check that uplink and call in the final coordinates for the extraction as soon as we reach the clearing."

"I think I can handle that," Moralez replied, and in a heartbeat, they were all up and moving along the rocky trail again.

In the Arabian Sea, under the cover of the high wind and rain, a Trident-Class nuclear submarine was patrolling off the coast of Iran. The sub commander turned off the comlink, after having received the order to launch his cruise missiles. He immediately ordered his personnel to battle stations. Sirens blared, lights flashed, and the crew scrambled around preparing for launch. After a final check, he gave word for them to fire at will. The first missile was propelled out of its launch tube by compressed air and broke the surface of the water. The cruise missile rocket engine ignited as it popped up out of the sea, sending the weapon streaking out into the horizon in a menacing blur. The same sequence of events repeated until all the launch tubes were empty.

All across the region, the coordinated ground, air, and naval attack against the Taliban in Afghanistan commenced. The precision strikes went on for several days.

It was time for some serious payback, the terrorists' turn to be terrified.

Early the following morning, back in Washington DC, the president and members of his cabinet reviewed detailed reports from the previous night's attacks on the Taliban.

General Smithfield also reported that the downing of the rogue airliner had been confirmed, and the resulting potential threat of the chemical explosion had the Iraqi government scrambling to the aid of its people. The Iraqis were eager to find out who was responsible for the devastating attack. Word from Intel in Iraq suggested that Iraqi leadership suspected U.S. involvement, or at least one of their allies.

The president turned to General Smithfield. "What about your insertion team? Do they have any intel about what the hell happened over there?"

Smithfield shuffled his feet nervously and fought the urge to bite his lip as he stood before the commander-in-chief. "We have been in contact with Light Force, Mr. President, and they confirmed the takeoff of the aircraft from a remote location in Iraq. They also reported contact with hostile terrorist insurgents. We are waiting for them to call in for extraction."

"And why are we waiting?" the president asked, the frown never leaving his face. "We need to get those men out of there now! Afterward, I want a full report on my desk, with all the data on this situation. I'm going to need it when the fingers start pointing about who is to blame for the alleged attack on Iraq."

"Yes, sir," Smithfield said, then took his leave, feeling the pressure was on him to get moving. He didn't want to be the last one standing when the music stopped. As soon as he was back in his office, he called into the Cy-Com Center and asked for Agent Foster.

Rob and his team had finally reached the small clearing along the side of the rocky ridgeline trail. They were exhausted from the long hike and the burden of carrying their gear and the body of their lost man. Moralez drained his canteen and passed out some rations.

Josh wiped the sweat off his face with his good hand, then turned to Adams. "I need something for pain, man. My shoulder is starting to throb again."

"No problem, buddy," Adams said, then pulled out the medical pack and gave Josh two pills. As Josh washed the medication down with some water, Adams tended to his wound with some more disinfectant and applied fresh bandages.

Tex checked the surrounding area with his field glasses and, to his disbelief, spotted Binfudi and his men heading in their direction, quickly making their way down the ridgeline trail they had just hiked. "Damn it! We've got some company coming again!" he yelled.

Rob took the field glasses from Tex and gasped when he saw the terrorists approaching from a distance. "How many of them are there anyway?"

"I dunno may five or six," Tex fumed. "They're like fuckin' cockroaches. For every one we kill, there are a dozen more scurrying around in the damn cracks."

"I want a claymore set about 100 yards back on the trail," Rob said to Moralez and Tex. "We'll need to hold off on that extraction call till we take care of this, uh...little problem. Everyone else, stay down and out of sight. Short bursts only, boys. We need to conserve ammo, since these guys keep comin' out of the woodwork. Hold fire until you hear me fire my weapon."

Light Force quickly moved into action. Morales and Tex crept backward, keeping low and carefully setting the claymores and tripwires alongside the trail. Everyone just made it back into position as Binfudi and his terrorists closed the gap. The men at the forefront of the enemy procession easily tripped the wire, and the claymores exploded into a ground-shaking detonation. Rob gave the hold signal to his team, but his nerves lingered on edge as he waited.

The terrorists in front of the evil parade were killed instantly in the hailstorm of metal fragments, Amwa Binfudi included. A few survivors were knocked off their feet and severely shaken from the shockwave of the blast.

They managed to get back on their feet and started hobbling along again, but as soon as they came into view and range, Rob let his nervous finger pull the trigger, and the fireworks began. Caught by surprise, most of the terrorists were cut down in the deadly, accurate gunfire.

The small remnant scattered into the ridgeline and started returning fire with whatever weapons they had. Tex loaded his launcher and fired at the enemy, lobbing grenades, one after another, in quick succession.

Adams moved to firing position and began peppering the trail with machinegun fire until his clip was empty. An AK round slammed into his arm as he was trying to reload his weapon, and he was knocked backward from the force of the impact. Despite the incoming gunfire, Rob moved to his comrade and dragged him to a safer spot as the rest of the team tried to cover them. Once Adams was under sufficient cover, Rob signaled for his men to hold fire.

Josh moved to Adams and grabbed the medical kit with his good arm. "Time to repay a little of that bedside manner," he mumbled. Adams was lucky, the bullet had glanced off his flak jacket and missed bone as it grazed the flesh of his upper forearm.

"Keep an eye on the trail," Rob instructed Moralez and Tex. Suddenly, the incoming gunfire stopped, and the few remaining terrorists ran for their lives, scurrying away like cowards. Rob could still feel the unique sensation of fear and excitement that could only come from a firefight.

Tex and Moralez returned after checking on the trail. "Just like the damn cockroaches to scramble when they get what they deserve," Tex said. "I don't see hide nor hair of anyone."

Rob turned to Josh. "Go ahead if you're up to it, put in the call, buddy. I want a one-way ticket outta this hellhole."

Josh put on the headset with his good arm and turned on the uplink. "Cen-Com, this is Light Force. I repeat, this is Light Force. Do you copy?"

Agent Foster, now on constant surveillance, quickly picked up the link. "Copy that, Light Force. We have your location on the uplink. What is your status? Copy?"

"We are more than ready for extraction, ma'am," Josh replied. "We've had enemy contact. Repeat, enemy contact! We're good for extraction ASAP. We've got two wounded and one KIA. Copy?"

"We copy that!" replied Foster. "Please leave your uplink on. Help is on the way."

As soon as the call was over, Foster told Stan Gustan to track the location of the troops. She was about to pick up the hotline to give Central Command a call, but General Smithfield beat her to it. "Agent Foster here," she said when she answered the incoming call.

"Agent, this is General Smithfield. You got any news for me? The president's on my ass."

"Actually, General, I do. We just heard from Light Force with those extraction cords."

"Good. Give 'em to me," Smithfield said, ready to keep the call short, as he knew time was of the essence. He needed to place the orders to set the extraction in motion, and he needed to do it quickly.

Every cog in the wheel worked in perfect synergy, and the extraction request reached the Fifth Fleet. The commander of a U.S. Naval aircraft carrier had orders in no time. The crew and the extraction teams were immediately placed on high alert, and everyone on the flight deck scrambled to prepare the Night Hawk helicopters. The extraction teams consisted of three Navy SEALs, a pilot, and a co-pilot/medic for each chopper. They were eager to get underway, so they hurriedly gathered their gear and loaded onto the waiting aircrafts. The pilots received the go-ahead from the crew after a quick pre-flight check, and the high-tech choppers lifted off, accelerated over the rolling waves, and disappeared into the foggy mist of the sea.

Chapter 16

Revenge

In the remote, mountainous region of Afghanistan, Special Operations teams were inserted close to a known Taliban stronghold. Brilliant flashes illuminated the horizon as the attack on the terrorists and their infrastructure continued. With the cover of darkness closing in around them, the teams dispersed into cover with quick precision. The rugged, unforgiving terrain made for slow going, but the troops were focused and determined to accomplish their mission.

As they drew closer to their targets, there was another bright flash of light out on the eastern horizon. As part of the ongoing attack to disable terrorist communications and infrastructure, a high-voltage power station was struck by a cruise missile. The resulting arch flash explosion was hotter than the surface of the sun, and the powerful blast leveled the power station and the surrounding area. Then, in the middle of the night, Special Ops teams began the final phase of their assault. With the element of surprise on their side, they valiantly attacked various terrorist bases, with a load of payback on their minds.

Stateside, Ashley had just returned home from a busy day at work in the city. She was sitting on the terrace, having a cup of tea and looking at her photo album. She missed Rob desperately and had begun to worry that she might never see his handsome, smiling face again. She desperately hoped she'd hear from him soon, but in the meantime, it did seem to be of some comfort for her to look at the pictures of their good times together. She prayed for Rob every night and clung to her hope that she would soon see him again, home safe and in her arms.

As far as Rob was concerned, their extraction couldn't come soon enough. Adams and Josh were holding up fairly well. Their wounds had stopped bleeding, and they were eating again. Rob thought that was a good sign of recovery.

"Yeah, anybody who can stomach these shit-in-a-bag MREs has gotta have a strong constitution," Tex joked as he finished his meal and started up the trail. On lookout,

Tex scanned the area with his binoculars, while the rest of the team set about defending the landing zone.

As his men toiled away, completely capable in their own right, their leader sat alone, staring at the picture of Ashley that he kept in his pack. Rob missed her, especially the smell of her hair and her warm smile that could always brighten his day. He wondered how his family was doing and how the city's recovery was coming. There were so many unanswered questions, but he wouldn't have his answers till he got back home.

The rescue choppers, with a firm lock on the uplink signal, cleared the coast and headed inland. They moved low and fast as they made their way into a large, sandy valley.

Unbeknownst to Rob and his troops, though, another group of fanatical terrorists were closing in, escorted in the back of an old transport truck and heading in the direction where heavy gunfire had been reported. They received word of the Americans from the one of the wounded terrorists who had escaped the firefight, and they were en route to enact the revenge they so loved. What they weren't aware of was that the extraction team had spotted them.

By the time the terrorists realized their journey was going to be cut short, the Night Hawks were already closing in on them from behind. The terrorists in the back of the truck began firing wildly at the incoming choppers. The order was given, and the gunner in the lead chopper opened fire with his mini-guns, killing all the truck occupants instantly as the rickety vehicle exploded in a yellow-orange fireball. The Navy SEALs and crew aboard the choppers broke out in cheer as the pilots made a wide, sweeping turn, gaining altitude. Everyone onboard was eager to get the job done, and they were getting ever closer to the coordinates on the uplink signal.

About fifty miles north of Rob and his team, a field hospital was set up on the outskirts of the area of the plane crash and devastating explosion. The Iraqi army was onsite to handle the incredible number of casualties caused by the explosion and chemical weapons.

At the site of impact, a team of army chemical specialists were sifting through the wreckage, looking for any clue that might reveal who was responsible for the horrible attack against the Iraqi people. They were fully covered from head to toe, dressed in oxygenated environmental suits as they moved through the carnage.

On their way out of the quarantine zone, one of the specialists spotted something sticking out of the sand. Upon closer examination, he discovered it was a dented heavy metal case that must have been blown clear of the blast. He quickly cleared the danger zone and cut the lock to open the case. To their surprise, it contained the personal documents of those individuals who had occupied the plane. The evidence was examined, and it was determined that Taliban terrorists were, in fact, out on a suicide mission to attack America. The explosion-proof case was on the plane for a reason: The twisted terrorists *wanted* the victims to know who was responsible.

The Iraqi president was quick to be informed about the disturbing contents of the case, and he was furious. In a public address to the people of Iraq, he openly condemned the terrorists for the death and destruction they were responsible for. He ordered all his military forces to seek out and destroy the Taliban. As fate would have it, just like that, the president of Iraq had joined in the fight against terrorism.

General Smithfield hurried to meet with the president, eager to share the news about the satellite images of the impact area in Iraq, which he'd just received from Agent Foster. He also had a video disc of the Iraqi president's speech to the people of his nation.

In the Oval Office, the president and the secretary of state were having coffee when Smithfield walked in and handed the president the Intel. Handshakes were exchanged, and everyone quickly took a seat.

The president took the manila envelope from Smithfield but first asked, "Any word on *my* troops in Iraq?"

Smithfield has an uneasy feeling, especially since the president insisted on emphasizing his "my." He took a deep breath to calm himself, then answered, "The extraction is in progress, sir. We have a lock on their uplink, and the extraction team is closing in."

"Good! I am happy to hear it," the president replied as he opened the envelope and scanned through the contents. He passed the images to his secretary of state and asked, "What's on the disc?"

"I'm not sure yet, sir. I haven't broken the seal on it, but Agent Foster insisted we should watch it ASAP."

"Well, in that case, let's get to it," the president said. He then picked up the phone and ordered an assistant to bring the disc player and display to his office.

The secretary of state finished staring at the images of chaos and destruction and spoke directly to the president. "Sir, I don't even want to think about the damage that plane would have inflicted on our people. Thank God the terrorists plot was stopped."

The president and the others remained quiet as they watched the video. When it was over, he turned to his secretary of state and ordered, "I want the video and images released to the press immediately. The American people need to know what the terrorists wanted to do to us."

The secretary gathered up the Intel. "A brilliant idea, Mr. President," she said. "They have the right to know."

With that said, the president ended the meeting, but not before thanking Smithfield, and reminding him how important it was to bring his troops back home.

Chapter 17

Realities of War

Rob and his team sat in their hideout next to the landing zone, waiting for their ride.

Moralez couldn't seem to stop staring at the body bag that contained Phil Takis. Tears filled his eyes and ran down his face as the reality of his friend's death began to take its toll. "We went through basic together," he said to Rob. "Phil was a damn good man, and now he's gone. He's got two kids back home, for God's sake!" Moralez struggled to regain his composure, then continued, "How can we tell them they're gonna grow up without their father?"

"It could have been any of us," Rob replied, moving closer to console his comrade. "I'm just as upset as you are about losing Phil. It's hard for me to believe he's actually in that damn bag. I wish it woulda turned out differently, Moralez. We all do, but death is the gamble we all take, every time we go out on a mission. Phil knew the risks, but he came anyway. So, yeah, you're right about him being a damn good man."

"Rob's right," Tex chimed in. "We all feel it when we lose somebody." He took a sip of water and looked away from the body bag, ready to change the subject. "I still don't understand why that damn plane didn't go down. The claymores shoulda taken it out."

Rob stood and looked each of his men in the eye. "We all did our best here, boys. None of us could have predicted that the claymores wouldn't stop the plane or that the uplink would fail at that critical moment. Right now, we just need to stay focused and get our butts out of this godforsaken place. That's what Phil woulda wanted."

"Hey, Tex," Adams shouted, "my damn shoulder is killing me, man. I need another shot."

Tex opened the medical kit and looked Adams over. He could see that he was shaking with pain, so he quickly handed over two pills. In a matter of minutes, the trembling stopped, and Adams was smiling, his face lightened from the powerful effect of the drugs.

Tex turned to Josh. "How 'bout you, kid? You doin' okay?"

Josh smiled. "I'm all right for now. No pills. I wanna stay frosty for the extraction."

Rob continuously scanned the area with his field glasses, but he somehow missed the lone terrorist crawling along the opposite ridge, slowly moving closer to them. The terrorist, on the other hand, certainly saw him. He was one of Binfudi's men, and he had an RPG strapped over his shoulder that he intended to use to avenge his comrades, as soon as he was within range.

"Incoming!" Josh suddenly yelled. "I've got a blue light blinking. I think our ride's here, boys."

Before Rob could reply, the unmistakable thumping started in the distance; the choppers were inbound to the LZ.

In the remote mountains of Afghanistan, Special Operations teams were bristling with weapons as they began their attack on a large terrorist compound. Caught by surprise, the terrorists scrambled to react to the firestorm of automatic weapons, but they had little chance of surviving it. The few remaining retreated into a large brownstone building, hoping to hide long enough to make their escape.

American Special Forces easily fought their way through the compound and surrounded the buildings. The shooting slowed, then stopped as they entered the brownstone and started their sweep. They had no idea that the tall, bearded terrorist, their prime target, had managed to slip out of the compound just seconds before it was surrounded; he and his assistant were now running for their lives. For the terrorists still in the brownstone, it was a fight to the death; Special Forces cleared every room and passageway in a matter of minutes.

Unfortunately for the U.S. forces, the ensuing victory came at a cost. Three men were killed in action, and four were critically wounded. By the time the entire compound was cleared, a total of forty-three terrorists were down, and ten wounded ones were captured. A large amount of Intel was seized, including several cell phones and hard drives.

The mission was a success, even though their main target was nowhere to be found.

Meanwhile, all across Afghanistan, the attacks by air and ground forces continued, striking a devastating blow to the evil that wanted to take over the world.

Rita Moralez's parents were thrilled to receive a call from her nurse, letting them know there was good news and that they should stop in to visit Rita immediately. The nurse wouldn't give them many details over the phone, but they could hardly wait to see what the call was about. Full of excitement, the Moralezes stopped their breakfast and made a mad dash to the city. In a matter of minutes, they had left their Newark, New Jersey apartment behind and were on the Amtrak.

They disembarked the train and practically ran the four blocks to City Hospital. After they checked in at the front desk, they saw Rita's nurse approaching, with a big smile on her face.

"The doctors are calling it a miraculous recovery," the nurse said as she led them to Rita's room.

This time, Rita was sitting all the way up, leaning back on her pillow. There were even fewer machines and tubes around her than before, and her complexion looked much better. Full of joy, Rita's mother moved to her daughter's side and took her by the hand.

Rita's eyes gradually opened, and a smile crossed her face. "Mama!" she squealed, embracing her dear mother.

Everyone in the room, even the nurse, was overcome with emotions, and tears of joy began to flow. There was happiness in the family again, and they were thrilled that they would not have to bid Rita goodbye after all.

There was a knock at the doorway, and the doctor stepped in. His smile widened as he took in the happy reunion. "Well, well! It's good to see that my favorite patient has some company this morning." After he shook hands with all of them, he moved to Rita's bedside. He checked her vitals carefully and asked her to squeeze his fingers as hard as she could. He pulled down Rita's blanket and touched her feet. "Can you feel that?" he asked as he ran his fingertips over her toes.

"Yes, a little," she replied.

"Good," the doctor replied. "What about moving your toes? Can you wiggle any of them?" The doctor smiled when he noticed some slight movement. "You, my dear, are improving. Keep up the good work!" He turned to find Rita's parents in tears again and left, still wearing that big, satisfied smile on his face. He had seen such a miracle only once before during his career, and that was when he was an intern, many years before.

Rita's father thanked God as he tried to compose himself. He wiped the tears from his face as he leaned down close to her and took her hand. "We are so proud of you, baby girl, and you're doing great. What can we do for you?"

Rita smiled. "Papa, I'd love my cell phone, a big cheeseburger, a Coke, and some fries. I also want to see my brother. Where is Jimmy? Is he okay?"

"He's on active duty, sweetie," Rita's mom replied. "He had to go, but Jimmy writes often. He has asked about you."

"Okay, Mom, but make sure he calls me soon."

"I am sure he will, as soon as he can."

Rita yawned, overcome by the powerful medicine she laid back on her pillow. Before long, her eyes fluttered shut, but she went to sleep with a sweet smile on her face. Her parents were so happy they could have screamed as they left to hunt down some fast food for their hungry daughter.

At the White House, the president was in a meeting with his secretaries of defense and state. They had been closely following the assault on Afghanistan and were encouraged by the reports coming of the success of air, ground, and naval forces. Taliban support and their defense infrastructure had been badly crippled. The reports also showed that a considerable amount of intelligence had been gathered, along with several high-ranking terrorists. While there were some American and ally casualties, there were very few by comparison. On the down side, their main target had somehow given them the slip.

The president's chief of staff entered the office and handed the president a stack of morning papers.

The president's face widened into a grin as he looked at the front page of *The Washington News*. He bolted to his feet and read the front headline out loud: "'Deadly Plane Heading for America Downed in Daring Attack by U.S. Special Forces!'" The president happily slapped the paper down on his desk and continued, "It is all working out as planned, with the exception of the capture of the terrorist leader." He then took his seat again and sipped his coffee, smiling over the brim of his cup that bore the presidential seal.

"Sir," his chief of staff said, "The Iraqi president has declared war on any remaining terrorist assets in Iraq. The amount of damage from that plane is just…unbelievable. The Iraqi military is on the move as we speak."

"Very well. Thank you," the president said, then dismissed him from his office.

The Oval Office was suddenly very quiet and very still, the president was deep in thought as he continued to drink his morning pick-me-up. Finally, he turned to his staff and said, "It seems we have a new ally in the war against terrorism. We must use this to our advantage." He turned to his secretary of state. "Offer our assistance to the Iraqi people. Also, please arrange a meeting with the Iraqi ambassador. I wish to offer our support to the victims of the plane crash. We must let the people know just how fanatical these terrorist are. We owe a lot to the men of Special Operations, Light Force in particular."

"Yes, Mr. President," the secretary of state said, quickly jotting down notes.

The president then turned to his secretary of defense. "Any word on their extraction?"

Caught off guard, Secretary Moreland struggled for the right reply. "I have to make a few calls, sir, but I am sure everything is proceeding according to plan."

The smile quickly disappeared from the president's face. "You're sure? How can you be sure if you haven't made those calls yet? I need answers, Moreland, and I need them now!" the president said, pounding a fist lightly on his desk. "Those men are our heroes, and I want our boys back on American soil. Now go!"

After they walked out, the president picked up his coffee mug again and quickly thumbed through the papers.

At Central Command, Smithfield received a call from Defense Secretary Moreland, who was clearly not happy. Smithfield felt the rope tightening around his neck, so he again placed a call to Agent Foster at Cy-Com. *As always, the shit runs downhill,* he silently seethed as he waited for her to pick up.

Rob and his team listened to the whirring of the choppers as they got closer and closer. Suddenly, as if magically appearing from the clouds, the sleek, black and green aircrafts popped up over the ridgeline, almost directly over them. As they banked into a wide turn, Josh fired a smoke grenade into the clearing. The chopper pilots spotted the smoke, and one of them started his approach into the landing zone.

The lone terrorist was within range but was waiting for the right moment to fire his deadly weapon at the chopper that was quickly descending. He was certain the RPG would take out the helicopter. *Even if I cannot kill them all, I will send some of them to their deaths today!* He thought with a snide smirk on his face.

Suddenly, a white streak flashed from somewhere on the opposite ridgeline, and Rob spotted it out of the corner of his eye. "Incoming! Hit the dirt!" he yelled as the rocket blurred overhead and hit the tail of the Night Hawk about twenty-five feet above ground. Fortunately for the chopper and crew, the rocket went through the tail section before it detonated. The explosion that followed sent the copter spinning down, though, and it slammed hard into the ground as the engines shut down.

Shocked but quick with his reflexes, the second chopper pilot pulled up and out of range, circling overhead.

"Where the hell did that come from?" Tex yelled.

"I think from that ridge across from us," Rob answered. "Tex, we gotta get to that downed chopper. Josh, you and Moralez cover us. Fire on that ridgeline. We've got a damn sniper with a rocket launcher!"

Josh and Moralez move into position, and the cover fire started. Rob and Tex stayed low as they ran for the downed chopper. The Navy SEALs in the hovering helicopter were determined to locate the attacker hiding in the rocks.

The terrorist made his final mistake when he moved to fire on the downed chopper again. He was frightened and in a hurry when he fired haphazardly, trying to avoid the bullets whirring and snapping around him, and his launched rocket missed its mark, streaking over the downed chopper and exploding against the rocky hillside. Pieces of rock and debris showered down on Tex and Rob as they struggled to open the side door of the Night Hawk.

The chopper above had a bird's-eye view of the place the rocket had been launched from, so they unleashed a barrage of rocket and cannon fire on that location, killing the shooter instantly in the massive explosions.

Rob and Tex peered through the windows and saw the troops inside. Together, using all their might, they managed to pry open the steel door. The SEALs had already placed their pilot on a stretcher; his head was bleeding, and his face was banged up from the crash. The co-pilot was still strapped in his seat, not moving. The SEALs handed the injured pilot off to Tex and Rob and moved to work on the co-pilot. In just a few moments, they had him out of his seat and placed carefully on another stretcher, all while he flailed about and screamed in pain, likely from his leg that was obviously shattered.

Josh and Moralez kept their eyes on the ridgeline as everyone scrambled across the landing zone. The remaining Night Hawk descended, and the SEALs jumped out and moved to assess the situation.

Rob stepped forward and greeted them. "Man, it's good to see you guys. Thanks for sticking your necks out to help us."

A tall, rugged-looking Navy SEAL stepped forward to shake his hand. "Lt. Howards, at your service." He looked around at the team. "Just so you know, we woulda walked if we had to. We won't leave anyone behind."

"I think we can all agree on that, Lieutenant," Tex said with a smile and a nod of his head.

"Didn't expect your rocket man over there though."

"Neither did we," Rob said.

One of the SEALs was a field medic, so he quickly broke open his medical kit and began treating the wounded while Rob and Lt. Howards reviewed their situation and worked to come to a mutual decision of what should be done. Ultimately, they determined that the two wounded pilots and Rob's KIA, along with his wounded, would head back on the working chopper with one of the Navy SEALs. The remaining SEALs would stay with Light Force until another extraction could be arranged.

Lt. Howards turned on their comlink and put in a call to the aircraft carrier. Considering that there was another band of fanatical terrorists heading their way, it was a wise decision. The working chopper was loaded and quickly headed up and away. Rob was glad to know that some of them would be out of harm's way. Phil was gone, but his body didn't deserve to rot in the nasty desert along with the bodies of the fanatical terrorists who had killed him.

Handshakes and high-fives were exchanged and

introductions made as the SEALs and Light Force joined together. A defensive perimeter was set up around the landing zone, and Tex and a SEAL sniper headed up to higher ground to keep watch for anymore stragglers.

Chapter 18

Extraction

The admiral of the aircraft carrier received the disturbing news of the downed chopper and immediately ordered the launch of another Night Hawk team, along with two fighter jets to provide escort. The ship deck exploded into action as the mighty carrier turned into the wind and readied for launch. The admiral used the comlink to make a call to headquarters, wanting to keep them in the loop about the situation in Iraq.

It was four in the morning when Smithfield's phone rang. Half-asleep, he scrambled to pick it up. He was disturbed to find out that the extraction hadn't gone smoothly, but he was more upset to know that some of his troops were still on the ground in Iraq. He hung up the phone, rubbed his throbbing temples, put on some coffee, then headed for the shower. It felt like there was a fist twisting his stomach as he imagined what the president would do to him if he found out his team didn't make it.

"Damn you, Rob! Get those boys outta there…or it's my ass too!" he muttered as the shower water ran over his body, doing very little to soothe him.

The Night Hawks had cleared the deck of the aircraft carrier, and two F-16 fighters were waiting for takeoff. The flight crew leader gave the go, and the mighty jets thundered down the deck and streaked out over the rolling sea, moving toward the inbound Night Hawks. The troops onboard had made a vow to their commander, promising that they would not come back without all men onboard, no matter what. Out over the sea, the fighter jets pulled alongside the Night Hawk choppers, and together, they headed for the coast.

Ashley turned down the invitation to join her co-workers for a few drinks. It was a rainy, dreary evening in the city, weather that mimicked her mood, and she didn't want to be a spoilsport. She opened her umbrella, headed down into the subway, and boarded her train for the lonely ride back to Jersey City.

Ashley was so worried about Rob that thoughts of him had begun to consume her mind day and night. His missions never bothered her before. She thought it might have been women's intuition, but whatever it was, she couldn't stop the nagging feeling that something was definitely wrong. Her anxiety over the matter had gotten so bad that she even told her mother about it over lunch. Her mother was a great comfort to her, as always, but even her consoling words did little to take the edge off her worry for long. On the ride home, she tried to think more positively, to concentrate on her faith in Rob, her blessings, and good memories, but as soon as she opened the front door of their condo, a feeling of dread washed over her every day. Distracting herself with work and volunteering on the weekends had helped to ease the worry some, but the longer she went without hearing from Rob, the harder it was to try to find a way to hold on to her hope.

Ashley stopped at the corner market on the way home and picked up some takeout for dinner. She would again eat alone, with nothing but her clinging hope to keep her company. Hope, love and prayers for Rob were all she really had, the only things that kept her going. The stories in the newspapers spoke of heroic acts by valiant American soldiers, but somehow, that only made her feel worse.

Across the Hudson, Rita Moralez continued her miraculous recovery at City Hospital. With the help of her doctors and hours of therapy, she had regained partial use of her lower body. Rita worked hard, dreaming of the day when she would once again walk on her own. Her family came to visit often, and everyone was elated about her amazing recovery. At times, Rita wondered where her brother was and how he was doing. She was proud of him for being a U.S. Army man, but she missed her big brother Jimmy and prayed she'd see him soon.

As it moved around in the Arabian Sea, the aircraft carrier picked up the Night Hawk on the comlink. The inbound chopper was headed their way. The admiral gave the order, and within a matter of minutes, all hands were on deck, awaiting the arrival of the rescue chopper. The sleek Night Hawk appeared in the horizon and soon made a pass directly over the mighty ship. The chopper swung into a wide turn and was directed down onto the gently rolling flight deck by the flagmen. As soon as the pilot killed the engine, the doors opened, and a swarm of troops rushed to their assistance.

The admiral watched as the wounded were placed on more adequate stretchers. As he knelt down beside them, to welcome them to his ship, his hat was almost blown off his head from the rotor wash.

Everyone stood at attention and saluted as the body of Phil Takis was slowly carried across the flight deck. The wounded were carried below deck, into the Medical Center. The admiral looked out upon the foreign sea, with an ocean of tears brewing in his eyes, praying for his men and hoping there would be no more body bags.

On land, several terrorists jumped out of their truck and started climbing up the rocky ridgeline, moving in the general direction of the weapon fire they'd heard from the distance. It did not take long for them to discover the blood-covered, nearly decapitated body of Binfudi, along with several of his dead comrades. They searched for the weapons used by the deceased and eventually found them in a pile of busted-up junk.

The evil bunch made quick work of their looting and pilfering and was on the move again, making their way to the top of the trail. There, they found more dead bodies, empty shell casings, and ammo clips scattered about. The yearning for bloody revenge festered in their dark hearts, and they moved more slowly now, searching along the trail and heading in the general direction of the landing zone in the distance. They hoped to surround the enemy and catch them in an ambush, as per their usual *modus operandi*; however, they had no idea that they were about to collide with an elite fighting force that would be the stuff of their own nightmares. If they had known, they would have tucked tail and ran for their lives.

Out on the Iraqi coastline, the inbound Night Hawks, along with their fighter escorts, were moving inland, flying low to stay off the radar. They continued tracking the uplink, using those coordinates to navigate them over the rugged, rocky terrain. One of the fighter pilots spotted the airstrip below, along with a large structure at the end of it. He confirmed the target and reminded himself to destroy it on the way out.

Back at the landing zone, everyone was anxiously awaiting the second extraction. When a call came in on the comlink, Moralez grabbed the headset and listened as the Night Hawk pilot informed him that they were about ten minutes out. Moralez informed the pilot, "Just look for the red smoke on your way in!"

Rob was relieved to hear that help was mere minutes away. As they waited, he and Moralez kept a watchful eye on their surroundings with the field glasses.

Up at the lookout, Tex spotted some movement in the distance. He scanned the trail with his high-powered spotting scope and, much to his dismay, picked up a group of figures moving in their direction, low and slow. Tex gave the SEAL sniper the range and firing coordinates. The SEAL steadied his big rifle and found his target in the crosshairs. He made one minor adjustment on his scope and lined up the shot.

Boom! Just like that, the lead terrorist was shot through the head and fell to the ground in a lifeless heap.

"Now *that's* a hit!" Tex yelled, clapping a hand on the sniper's shoulder in congratulations.

Quickly, the sniper zeroed his crosshairs in on someone else and fired again.

Boom! Another head shot dropped another terrorist.

Tex watched in awe as the remaining terrorists moved down out of sight, scrambling for cover. "Way to get 'em, cowboy," he said as he and his comrade picked up their gear and moved down to the landing zone. As soon as they reached the others, Tex informed Rob, "We're about to have more company. Jesse James here took out two with headshots, but there might be four or five of them suckers left."

"Head shots? Good. Those bastards deserved it. How far out are the others?" Rob asked.

"About 300 yards down the trail," Tex replied. "It looks like maybe they're on the run, but they might sneak on us."

Rob turned to Moralez, "Get on the uplink and let our people know there are hostiles on the trail. Maybe they can rain down a little fire and brimstone on the nasty bastards."

Moralez grinned, then grabbed the uplink and made the call. Within moments, the tell-tale chopping sound could be heard in the distance.

Lt. Howards keyed his radio and called the inbound Night Hawks. "Bravo, Bravo, do you copy? We've got the LZ secured, but we've got a few incoming hostiles. Repeat, hostiles on the ridgeline trail! Do you copy?"

"Copy that. Hostiles on the ridgeline. Be advised that an airstrike is coming your way. Mark your smoke. Copy?"

Howards keyed his mic. "We copy that, Bravo…and mark our smoke. The ridgeline is directly to the east of our mark."

On the lieutenant's nodded command, one of the SEALs fired two smoke grenades out into the east corner of the landing zone. Everyone hunkered down in the cover, waiting for the coming airstrike.

The Night Hawks slowed while the F-16 fighter jets broke formation and accelerated toward the ridgeline. The fighters searched the ridgeline with their infrared scanners and picked up the heat signatures of the hiding terrorists. The mighty jets swung into a wide, sweeping turn, streaking right over the landing zone. The pilots lined up the targets and launched their lancer missiles along the ridgeline trail, then quickly pulled up and away from the huge, ground-shaking explosions. The terrorists were killed instantly as a huge firestorm of death covered the side of the ridgeline.

Rob and the teams literally jumped for joy as the sleek, silver jets swept over them and headed back to escort the Night Hawks.

"Yee-haw!" Tex cried. "Now get those big whirlybirds down here and get us the hell out!"

General Smithfield sat at his desk and poured himself another glass of aged scotch. His nerves were starting to wear on him, and he hoped the whiskey might do him some good. It was a lot of pressure, the weight of the president and his concern for his troops, as well as the waiting and not knowing if his team was safely out of Iraq. No matter how much he drank, he couldn't seem to silence the president's last words that haunted him: *"I want our boys back on American soil."*

Smithfield took a big gulp of his scotch and glanced at the phone on his desk. There was nothing he could do now but hope it would ring with good news. The warmth of the scotch flowed through him as he sat, deep in thought. It was, as always, up to the troops to get the job done, and Smithfield chuckled at the irony. "They're over there with those hostiles all around them, and over here, it's my ass that's on the line."

Rob and Lt. Howards deployed their teams around the landing zone as the choppers came into view in the distance. The SEALs had set high explosives inside the downed chopper; they would use a remote detonator to destroy it once everyone was clear. The fighters swept over the ridgeline, scanning the trail one last time, then streaked directly over the landing zone again. Rob felt the hairs on the back of his neck stand up as he took in the sight of the mighty jets.

The chopper pilots spotted the red smoke below and began their approach. The first Night Hawk to appear over the ridgeline lowered onto the landing zone, and the second touched down in a cloud of dust from the rotor wash.

"Everyone, move out!" Rob yelled over the noise. "Get onboard now!"

No one had to be told twice, and the teams quickly split up and jumped into the waiting choppers. Rob looked over his men as the chopper began to lift off. For the first time in a long time, he saw smiles on their faces.

"Damn, I hate flying in these things," Tex complained.

"I'm sure the pilot will set you back down if you want," Rob chided.

"What!? Hell no! I'd hitch a ride in the mouth of a Great White to get the hell outta this shithole."

"Roger that!" Rob replied with a grin. "For a while, I was beginning to have my doubts that we'd make it, but I guess we pulled through."

Moralez turned to Tex, wrinkling his brow in confusion. "Man, I'm glad we're getting out, but I still can't believe that plane made it off the freaking runway."

"Believe me, I know how you feel," Tex replied. "I know we set those claymores just right. But anyway, at least we kicked some terrorist butt out there."

"We did shoot 'em up pretty good, huh?" Moralez replied, "I keep thinking about Rita. I pray she made it. Matter fact, I pray for all the people of NYC."

Rob smiled. "We kicked some ass all right. I figure we nailed at least fifty of those crazy suckers. As for the Big Apple, I pray for the victims, their families. The American people are nothing if not resilient, and they tend to pull together. I'm sure Rita's fine and that the city's getting back in operation again. I do wonder how things are back home though," Rob said. "I miss my lady, my family. I hope our military took out that plane before it reached its target."

The co-pilot, who just so happened to be listening in, got up and left the cockpit. "I'm Sergeant Zinski. Everyone calls me Zink."

Handshakes were offered, along with thanks from the team.

"We really can't thank y'all enough," Tex said. "The terrorists where coming at us from everywhere. I just wish we coulda stopped that big bird."

Zink smiled, unable to hold the good news back a moment longer. "You really have no clue, do you?"

"No clue about what?" Rob asked.

"You guys are heroes! Hell, it is front-page news back home. That deadly plane heading for America was downed in Iraq by a daring U.S. Special Forces attack. It's all over the papers."

Tex jumped up. "No shit? You're foolin', jerkin' our chains, right?"

"Nope. I'm serious, my friends," Zink added, still smiling. "A big spread, about ninety miles from your landing zone, was devastated by an enormous chemical blast when the plane went down. The thing left a big ol' scar on Iraq, that's for sure."

Moralez jumped up and stood next to Tex, gawking at Zink. "Oh my God! I... We did it!" he said, glancing over at Tex. "Now that's some serious kick-ass!"

Zink's expression grew somber. "It's a shame that thousands of Iraqis died from the chemical blast. The Iraqi military is really pissed off, so much so that they've vowed to fight the terrorists here, on their own soil."

The conversation ceased for a moment as the realization struck home. Innocent people had been slaughtered again, and it didn't really stifle the pain to know they were people in another part of the world. More women and children, young and old, had died, all because of terrorist foolishness by people of their own nation.

Rob stood before his men. "It wasn't our fault, you guys," he said. "Listen up! It was those damn terrorists who opted for chemical warfare. We did our job. We had to take the plane down. I'm sorry for all those deaths, but if we didn't do our jobs, they would have killed people anyway. They were killers, and we had to destroy them."

"You're right, Rob," Tex said, as his mood lightened a bit. "We wouldn't have even been there if not for those evil bastards."

Moralez added, "Yeah, we didn't start this crap. It was them, and we did the best we could to clean up their damn mess...again."

Airman Zinski shook hands with everyone, went back to the cockpit, and took his seat. Before long, things quieted down. Rob sat back and felt as if a giant weight had been lifted off his shoulders. They were finally heading home, and their mission was a success after all. He tried not to think about what it would have been like if the plane had hit America.

As the choppers accelerated toward the coastline. One of the fighters broke formation and headed back for the enemy base. The jet pilot aligned his aircraft with the runway and released a barrage of missiles. The first group hit the runway, and the others slammed directly into the hangar. The fighter pilot then pulled up into a sweeping turn as the runway and hangar exploded below him.

The formation continued moving over the coast, and the chopper pilot keyed his radio. "Com-1, Com-1! Bravo! I repeat, Bravo! We are inbound. Copy?"

An officer on the bridge scrambled to grab the mic. "We copy that, Bravo! Bravo is clear for approach!"

The admiral was below deck when the all-hands alarm rang out through the ship. In a matter of seconds, his phone was ringing. He hung up after a hurried conversation, full of excitement and headed for the deck. The admiral and his staff looked on as the incoming Night Hawks closed in for landing

Tex looked out the side window and saw the huge carrier in the distance, ready to welcome them aboard. The fighter jets broke formation and gained altitude as the choppers moved closer to the massive flight deck.

Rob looked down at the huge flight deck as the chopper lowered and touched down. At almost the same time, the other Night Hawk landed. The doors opened and the teams began to pile out. A long line of Navy sailors in white uniforms stood at attention as Rob and his team walked by. They were all introduced to Admiral McCall and his staff. Rob couldn't help but notice all the medals on the admiral's uniform as he smiled appreciatively at them.

"Welcome aboard, everyone, and congratulations on a job well done!" the admiral said.

Lt. Howards stepped forward and saluted. "All hands are present and accounted for, sir!"

The admiral smiled as he looked over their dirty, unshaven faces and their dust-covered, torn uniforms, sure signs that they'd been in combat on the ground. "Excellent job, Lieutenant," he commended. "We are delighted to see all of you safely onboard!"

The admiral shook their hands, then proceeded to introduce his officers to Rob, the lieutenant, and both teams. Cheers erupted from the sea of white uniforms as the SEALs and Light Force made their way through the receiving line stretched out across the flight deck.

"Admiral, may we have permission to visit our wounded comrades?" Rob asked as the noise died down.

"Of course! They are doing well, and they would be thrilled to see you. There will be plenty of time for that," The Admiral replied heartily.

The chief of the ship was named Wiley, and he was assigned to assist them with any requests they had during the voyage. All their weapons and gear were loaded into a large bin, and Rob and his team were escorted below deck. Rob was surprised to see how clean and organized the interior of the gigantic vessel was as they moved down a long corridor to get to their quarters. He was also pleasantly surprised to find clean uniforms laid out on their bunks for them.

"I am sure you guys can use a little downtime," Wiley said. "The shower room is right next door. I'll be back in a few hours. I know the admiral wants to sit down and talk with all of you."

"Thanks, Wiley," Rob replied as he looked around the large room, especially ogling the enormous table that was loaded with a buffet of all sorts of food and drink. "Damn, will you look at this place?"

"I don't know about y'all, but I think that food smells a lot better than those MREs...or you guys' sweat, for that matter," Tex said, inhaling the aromas wafting off the feast. "I think it's time for some proper grub, boys!"

Rob walked over and took a seat at the table, and everyone quickly dug into the hot meal, barely bothering to get a word in between bites as they stuffed their hungry faces. Once their stomachs were full, the team stripped out of their filthy clothes and enjoyed long, hot showers, washing off the combat grime and layers of sand stuck in unpleasant places.

With all the crud washed off of him, Rob stretched out on his bunk. The stressful mission was over, and that meant he could easily close his eyes and drift off, thinking of Ashley and her warm smile. Before long, the entire team was sound asleep.

There were a lot of people waiting for good news, including the president, so as soon as the uplink was ready, the admiral made a call to Washington.

Smithfield was in his office when his secretary burst in. "General," she said, "there's an urgent long-distance call for you on Line 1. It sounds pretty important."

Smithfield almost knocked the phone off his desk as he scrambled to pick up the receiver. He was flooded with relief when the admiral filled him in. Excited almost beyond words, he made a direct call to the president, and the few minutes it took for the man to get on the line were agonizing for the impatient general.

The president was beyond elated. "Call me when you have a firm time for their arrival," he said to Smithfield. "I'm so glad our boys are coming home!"

Smithfield hung up and leaned back in his seat, taking in the moment. He took another swig of scotch, albeit a celebratory one this time, even raising the glass in the air for an invisible toast.

Next on the agenda was to work out the details of the teams' return, so he called for a staff meeting in one hour.

The news spread quickly across the political and military grapevine, and Agent Foster was among the many who were thrilled to hear that their prayers had been answered. She was proud of Cy-Com and her part in the successful mission.

On the carrier, Rob awoke to the smell of coffee brewing and the clattering of one of Wiley's assistants, setting the table. He looked over at Tex, who was snoring away, then sneaked over to him and yelled, "Wake the hell up, soldier!"

Tex jerked awake and saw Rob grinning, staring at him from just inches away. "Goddamn it, sucker!" he whined. "You just wait. Turnabout's fair play, but payback's a damn bitch!"

Moralez couldn't help but burst out in laughter at their banter, especially when Tex threw his pillow at Rob, and Rob countered by chasing him with a bucket of toilet water.

It didn't take long for the others to dress and sit down at the table for coffee and a light breakfast, all of them laughing and enjoying much better times than they had in the past few days.

"I wonder if I can call home. I need to find out about Rita," Moralez said.

"That's a good question, Moralez. I sure would like to call Ashley. I'll ask the admiral."

Wiley arrived at their quarters and joined them for a quick cup of coffee. When everyone was ready, Wiley escorted them down through a labyrinth of hallways, to the Medical Center.

In Washington, the president had given authorization to his press secretary to spill the homecoming story to the media. All across the country, the heroic tale was told again about the Special Forces team that downed the deadly chemical plane destined to invade America with its toxic death. The president, like everyone else, was relieved that they were safe and homebound, as the nation was in dire need of positive news as they strived to get beyond the evils of the recent past.

The reporters grilled the press secretary for specifics about when and where they would be returning, but he held firm with the standard line: "That has yet to be determined."

In New York, Ashley stopped at her favorite coffee shop on the way to work. She picked up a newspaper and sat outside, reading the front-page headlines about the Special Forces team that was coming home. She had no idea that the news had anything to do with Rob, as the military always kept everyone in the dark about the details, so as to protect their troops. As she walked the busy sidewalk to enter her office building, she wondered where he was and how he was doing.

Rob and his team followed Wiley into the sprawling Medical Center. They stopped at the front desk, and a medical officer greeted them with a smile. After Wiley spoke to him for a moment, he led them to the end of another wide hall, then into a room full of beds. They found

Adams, Josh, and the SEAL pilots smiling at them from across the room.

"Well, well. You guys are looking much better," Rob acknowledged.

"Yeah, well, it helps that we've got a cutie taking extra-good care of us," Adams replied with a wink.

The SEAL co-pilot laughed as Josh added, "You'd swear the guy's in love with her, always lookin' at her like a little lost puppy dog."

They all broke into a round of laughs, teasing Adams relentlessly and completely unaware that the nurse was within earshot and staring at them.

"What's so funny?" the nurse said, sauntering up to them and wearing a warm smile. "I like a good joke myself," she said, looking coyly at Adams.

Instantly, he was caught in the gaze of her bright hazel eyes. For a moment, he was rendered speechless, until he finally blurted, "Uh, we, um... We were just kidding around."

"Yes, I know," she said. "Boys will be boys, no matter how old they are."

"How are Josh and Adams doing?" Rob asked.

The nurse smiled as she moved to Adams and checked his bandages. "The doctor opened their wounds and cleaned them out. They both are doing very well."

"Good," Rob replied.

The nurse walked over to the Navy SEALs and began to check them over.

"What about Phil?" Rob asked. "Where's his, uh…body?"

The nurse sensed a sudden change in mood as the room went quiet. "He's in the cooler right now," she said flatly.

Before Rob could say anything, Wiley cut in and reminded them it was time for their meeting with the admiral and his staff.

Rob turned to Josh and Adams. "I've got some good news for you guys. Our Claymores damaged the plane after all. It went down about ninety miles from our location."

"What!?" Josh said. "Now *that* makes me feel a whole

lot better."

"Yeah, well, the damn thing was loaded with high explosives and deadly chemicals. Thousands of Iraqis were decimated from the blast and the aftereffects of the toxins."

Adams shook his head and let out a groan. "I hate to say it, but thank God it went down before it hit home."

Tex smiled. "We're all heroes and didn't even know it!"

The mood lightened, and high-fives ensued before Rob, Tex, and Moralez followed Wiley to their meeting.

Chapter 19

Homeward

General Smithfield sat in a meeting with several high-ranking officials of the Army, Navy, and Air Force. They had worked out a plan for Light Force's return trip, coordinating with Admiral McCall. It was decided that as soon as the carrier entered the Persian Gulf, a helicopter would carry them to an Air Force base in Saudi Arabia. From there, a long-range transport aircraft would escort them to another airbase just outside Washington. The president would be there to greet them personally upon their arrival.

Since the news had broken about the homecoming of Light Force, the press had been driving everyone crazy with questions. The evening news networks offered extensive coverage as they put the pieces together concerning the mission; however, they still did not know the identities of the men who comprised Light Force, since all Special Operations had to be concerned with confidentiality.

The president did plan to release more to the press when the time was right, as he wanted the American people to join in the homecoming. Smithfield tried his best to talk him out of it, to which the president said, "After the horror of 9/11, a heroes' welcome will do everyone some good."

Onboard the aircraft carrier, Wiley escorted Rob and his team into the massive Command Center. One of the admiral's staff members greeted then at the entrance, and Rob noticed Lt. Howards and his SEAL team as he walked in. He also noticed a handful of naval officers standing at the table, grinning at them. Everyone took a seat at the long wooden table.

Admiral McCall soon arrived and offered a warm welcome as he stood before them. "I want to thank all of you for a job well done. It is unthinkable to even imagine what would have happened if that plane had hit home. I have some film from Cy-Com, and I would like all of you to see it for yourselves."

A large projector screen lowered, and the first image flashed across it.

"As you can see," McCall continued, "the impact crater is enormous."

The room quieted as all eyes stared at the incredible devastation from the chemical blast.

"The Iraq military is up in arms, ready to move against any terrorists who dare to remain in Iraq. We are in the process of providing aid to the Iraqi people."

A round of cheers broke out among the group.

"Everyone is very proud of all of you. We are about six hours away from the Persian Gulf. When we arrive, two of our Night Hawks will take you to our Saudi airbase. From there, you will board transport aircraft to head to another airbase just outside Washington. The president himself sends his regards, and he is eager to meet all of you." McCall then took his seat and looked around the table. "Do any of you have any questions?" he asked.

Rob stood at attention. "Sir, there are a few things on my mind."

"Go ahead lieutenant Marrino."

"Well, first, I'd like to thank Lt. Howards, his SEALs, and the Navy pilots for risking their lives to pull us out of a hot LZ. I don't know how much longer we could have held out with so many terrorists closing in on us. Also, sir, my team and I would like to know if we can call home and talk to family. We've been out of touch for some time. I'm sure they are worried about us."

McCall smiled. "Of course, Lieutenant. We can arrange that for you. You can use our comlink through Cy-Com. I will have Wiley escort you to our communications area at your convenience."

"Great. Thank you, sir," Rob replied, then took his seat.

Lt. Howards stood up next. He looked at the admiral only briefly before tuning his gaze on Rob. "It is always a great honor for us to help our combat troops in need." He paused a moment as a broad grin stretched across his face. "Hell, we woulda come in there on roller skates to get you out of that godforsaken place. It felt good to get a little payback on the bastards."

The meeting lasted another half-hour as Admiral McCall went through an informal debriefing on the details of the mission.

In the mountains of Iraq, a column of Iraqi mechanized infantry had finally made their way into the remote valley where the terrorist airbase was located. They had received reports from a nearby village about automatic weapons fire and explosions, and it had taken them hours to make their way through the rugged mountains of rock and sand.

The Iraqi military was looking for a fight, but it soon became apparent that they had missed the party; all they found were the bloated bodies of dead terrorists, busted-up weapons, and large, twisted pieces of a destroyed structure at the end of what appeared to be a makeshift runway.

Rob and his team were back in their quarters when they receive word from Wiley that the comlink was ready for their calls.

"Who wants to go first?" Wiley asked.

Rob pointed to Moralez, "You get the honors, my friend."

Moralez jumped up. "Thank you, sir! I pray there will be some news about Rita,"

"We can give you ten minutes a piece," Wiley said, pointing the way.

The team followed Wiley up to the next level and into the huge communications complex, full of electronic equipment. They took their seats next to a small room that was set up for them to make private calls. Wiley explained how the comlink worked and handed the headset to Jim Moralez. Full of excitement, Moralez took his seat in the little room and made his call to his sister.

Rita was home from the hospital, sitting up in bed and watching TV. She picked the phone up on the first ring and squealed in delight when she immediately recognized her brother's voice. She was so overcome with emotion that it took a moment for her to get the words out. "Jimmy! It's so good to hear your voice. H-How are you?" she asked hesitantly, as if she feared the answer.

On the other side of the line, Moralez was flooded with joy. "I'm okay, on my way home to see you! Never mind me though. What happened to you, baby girl? I've been so worried about you."

It took a moment for Rita to reply. "I-I was at work, in my office, and the next thing I knew, I was waking up in the hospital."

"Thank God you made it, little sister! I've been praying for this day, just to hear your voice again and to know you're all right."

The siblings spoke quickly, knowing their time was limited. Rita told him she had to sit in a wheelchair, but the doctors had assured her that she would walk again. When their call ended, all too soon for either of them, Moralez removed his headset and sniffled as the tears of joy continued to flow. It took him a moment to gather himself and tell his comrades his prayers had been answered, but everyone was happy to see a smile on his face again.

Rob was the last to use the comlink. He walked into the room, picked up the headset, and called Ashley. He got the answering machine at the condo, so he tried her work number.

Ashley was on the computer when her phone started ringing. She picked it up and just about jumped out of her chair when she recognized the voice on the line. "Oh my God! Rob? I've been so worried about you. Where are you?"

"I'm on a luxury cruise," he teased.

"I'm serious, Rob. Where?"

"On a gigantic aircraft carrier, in the Persian Gulf neighborhood. It's good to hear your voice again, baby. I will be home soon. How are things at home?"

Ashley was flooded with emotion as she replied, "It is so good to hear from you. I miss you! Everyone's okay, but your brothers have been asking about you. It's been hard, but things are slowly getting a little better in the city. I'm working from a new location now."

"Good," Rob replied. "It is good to hear you're back to work. I can't wait to see you and the family again."

Their call also felt too short, but Ashley hung up with a smile as the good news sank in. Rob was okay, on his way home, and she couldn't wait to tell his family what she'd learned.

After all the personal calls were made, Wiley led them back to their quarters, where Lt. Howards and his SEAL team were waiting for them. Rob noticed a large cooler filled with beer, as well as a box of expensive-looking cigars and more food on the table. It wasn't long before the beer cans started popping open.

Wiley smiled as he turned to leave. "If you guys wanna smoke, you'll have to go up on deck."

As soon as Wiley closed the door, Tex shook a beer can, popped it open, and sprayed it right in Moralez's face. Just like that, the boyish mayhem began. After an hour of wild celebration, Rob passed the word, and everyone helped to clean up the gigantic mess.

A few hours later, Rob, Tex, and Lt. Howards headed up on deck to enjoy their fine cigars. Rob was amazed at the size of the flight deck as he looked around and out to the endless blackness of the sea before them. The wind was calm, and the full moon was a big, bright ball in the sky; it seemed so close that Rob was sure he could reach out and touch it. The stars were out in all their glory, dazzling in the ebony dark velvet of night, their reflections glistening in the water like diamonds.

Tex lit up his rum-flavored cigar and smiled. "That was one helluva mission, gentlemen. It was mighty good to get some revenge for our fallen comrades and the civilians at home. I hate those terrorist bastards!"

Rob took a pull from his cigar. "It woulda been better if Phil was with us, but we did the best we could." He paused and glanced up at the stars again. "Just think how close we came. If that plane had gone down and blew up on the runway, we'd all be goners."

"Hey, I'm sorry you guys lost a man out there," Howards chimed in. "I've been through that shit before. It's rough."

Tex sipped his beer. "That's the chance we all take going into the shit. The important thing to remember is that the mission was a success. That plane went down before it reached America."

Rob raised his beer, and they both clanked their cans against his for a toast. "To the mission!" he said.

As they continued talking about home and enjoying their cigars, the all-hands signal blared. The flight deck exploded into action as the crews scrambled on deck. Rob watched in awe as two sleek attack jets rose up to the deck. They launched within minutes, heading out over the glassy surface of the sea. Their afterburners lit up the night sky as they pulled into a vertical climb. Out in the distance, a bright light flashed out of the sea and streaked up into the night sky. Another cruise missile was on its way. Tex smiled at Rob. "Payback really *is* a bitch!"

"Dinner's ready!" Rita's mom yelled from the kitchen.

Rita snapped out of her daydream, still thinking of her brother. She slowly climbed out of bed and slipped into her wheelchair. She made her way into the kitchen and found her father sitting at the table, smiling at her. Rita managed to stand and topple into her chair at the table; she insisted on doing things herself. So far, she had come a long way in her recovery. She could now stand on her own, but walking would take a while, even though the physical therapists were quite amazed by her progress thus far.

Her mom finished setting the table and took her seat. She folded her hands and began to bow her head and was just about to say grace when Rita interrupted with a smile. "What is it, dear?" she asked, looking at her daughter curiously.

"Make sure you throw extra thanks in there for the good Lord, Mama," Rita said.

"What? Why?"

"Because Jimmy just called a few minutes ago. He's on his way home!"

Rita's mom almost fell out of her chair, and her father raised his glass of beer high in the air, "Thank God! I was so worried about our Jimmy. Our prayers have been answered once again."

In time, the family settled down to eat, and Rita filled them in on the details of her phone call, still hardly able to believe she would see her brother soon.

The massive aircraft carrier had lurched to within range of the Night Hawk helicopters. The order was given, and the mighty ship dropped down from full speed and moved toward optimal range point. Below deck, after a cutthroat poker game with the Navy SEALs, Rob and the team were finally sound asleep.

After a few hours, the eastern horizon began to lighten as the sunrise painted the sea and the sky in a glorious array of blues, violets, oranges, and reds, the new day swallowing up the night.

As soon as Rob opened his eyes, he saw Wiley's smiling face looking right back at him. "It's time to get moving, gentlemen," Wiley said loudly, looking around the wrecked quarters, at the beer cans and dinner plates scattered all about. It was shocking enough to see in that condition, but he really would have been thrown for a loop if he had seen it prior to their so-called cleanup detail.

Rob looked at Wiley and winced. "God, my head is killing me. Do you have some coffee and maybe a few aspirin?"

Wiley nodded. "The coffee pot is waiting for you. Forget about the mess. You guys deserved some fun. You might want to get your crew up and ready though. You've all got a long day ahead of you."

Rob slowly got up and looked around. Moralez was awake, but Tex was still sleeping, snoring loudly. He struggled to hold in his laughter as he tiptoed over and poured a cup of ice water on Tex's face.

"What the hell?" Tex screamed, jumping up. Son-of-a-bitch! Not again!"

Rob turned on the lights, and more laughter ensued at Tex's expense. They only laughed harder when Tex began chasing Rob around the room in his underwear. It was the kind of thing only the best of friends could get away with, and they would continue to laugh about it for years. It took a while before everyone calmed down from their antics long enough to get cleaned up and sit down at the breakfast table.

Smithfield arrived at the Cy-Com Center for his staff meeting, eager to work out the final details for the Light

Force homecoming. The president would be visiting Cy-Com for the first time, and he wanted to make a good impression.

Agent Foster smiled as she greeted Smithfield. "Everything is set. The whole place is spotless, and the meeting room is ready." She gave Smithfield a tour of the sprawling facility before they arrived at the spacious meeting room.

Smithfield greeted many of his old friends, and then took a seat next to the Secret Service director, Sam Colin. The meeting lasted over an hour, but they managed to come to a general consensus as to how the homecoming and the president's visit should go.

Ashley was just finishing up the last details of the day before leaving work. She found it hard to concentrate, and she couldn't stop thinking about Rob, albeit in a happy way this time. He had been on other missions, but that one really had her worried. She was excited and relieved that her own personal hero was on his way back home. Finally, she finished up and rushed to catch her train for a ride across the Hudson. She looked out at the skyline of the city and found herself staring at the empty space that was once home to the Twin Towers. It was hard for her to accept that things would never be quite the same again. She still couldn't believe that any structures so enormous could just disappear, crumbling into a gigantic pile of steel, and concrete.

Ashley bought a warm pretzel to enjoy as she headed along the busy sidewalk. Back in her condo, she turned on the evening news and made herself a pot of tea. A special report came on about the attacks against the Taliban and the homecoming of a mission team. She had read the headlines in her morning paper about the deadly airliner being downed, but it hadn't occurred to her that Rob had really had anything to do with it. Now, he was on his way home, and the reporters were talking about a homecoming. "Could it be…him?" She asked aloud, then answered her own silly question with a shake of her head. "No. Couldn't be." She dismissed the idea with a laugh, changed the channel, poured herself a steaming-hot cup of tea, and found her favorite chair.

Back in the Persian Gulf, Rob and his team were getting ready for their trip to the Saudi airbase when Lt. Howards and his team stopped by for a visit. "You guys have a good trip home," Howards said. "You deserve it."

"What do you mean?" Rob asked, arching a brow at him. "You're coming with us."

"I'm afraid not, my friend. We've got another mission. We're heading out tomorrow morning."

"Well, that just means we can suck up all the glory," Tex said, unable to help himself.

Howards looked at Tex's smiling face. The room was quiet for a moment before everyone joined the two in laughter. Hugs and handshakes were passed out freely as the teams wished each other well.

"Time to get on deck, gentlemen," Wiley said, popping his head in the door. "The choppers are almost ready to go."

Rob and his men followed the Navy SEALs up to the flight deck. Admiral McCall greeted them, and they walked toward the waiting chopper. The uniformed Navy personnel had lined up again and stood at attention as they walked by. The flag-covered body of Phil Takis was carried onto the chopper first.

The admiral stepped forward and smiled as he looked at Rob and Lt. Howards. "Your country is proud of all of you. Have a safe trip home."

The teams then dispersed, and Rob led his into the waiting chopper. As soon as they were settled onboard, the chopper lifted off the deck and accelerated out over the rolling sea.

Josh smiled as he watched the carrier grow smaller and smaller, eventually fading in the distance. "We're on our way!" he yelled out.

"Thank the Lord," Tex said. "Hey, how's your shoulder?"

"Feeling better every day," Josh answered.

Rob looked at Adams. "What about you, buddy?"

"I'm good, but it's gonna be a while before I can lift any weight with the arm."

"Is that why you didn't carry that hot little nurse onboard with ya?" Tex teased.

For an answer, Adams just shook his head.

"There was a time when I thought we might not make it, but we pulled through," Moralez added with a smile.

"We sure as hell did, and we kicked some terrorist butt in the process," Rob said. "I just wish Phil were here to enjoy the moment, but somehow, I think he'll always be with us from now on."

The co-pilot broke the silence. "Everyone, buckle up tight. The weather up ahead looks a little rough."

At the Saudi airbase, they had just picked up the radar signature of the incoming Night Hawks, and a quick radio check confirmed their location, about fifteen minutes out and closing. Out on the airfield, the crew was busy prepping the transport for their long flight back home.

The Saudi airbase commander, Blair Davic, was a seasoned veteran of the Gulf war, and he knew Rob

Marrino, since they had served together during *Desert Storm*. Davic was briefed on the action in Iraq, and he was eager to reunite with his old friend and to meet the entire Light Force team. He wanted to personally congratulate them for taking out the deadly terrorist threat. When Davic received a call to tell him they'd picked up a visual on the choppers in the distance, he put on his hat and jacket and headed out front of their sizable headquarters building.

The Night Hawks broke into a wide turn and hovered over the landing zone. They touched down in a cloud of dust stirred up by the rotor wash. Rob and his team grabbed their gear and exited the chopper. They were instantly engulfed in the searing heat reflecting off the tarmac, and the glare of the sun was almost blinding.

They were escorted to a large, white van that carried them across the vast airbase. Tex looked out at the sand dunes in the distance as they drove toward a large, brick and steel building. He couldn't help but notice the crowd of uniforms out front as their driver pulled up and parked the van.

Base Commander Davic stepped forward and looked them over with a grin on his face. "We've been expecting you, old pal," he said, grabbing Rob's hand for a firm shake. "It's good to see you all."

"Thank you, sir! It's good to be back," Rob said, greeting his old friend with a smile.

"Come. Let us go inside and have some lunch. We have a lot to talk about."

Inside, Davic parted ways for a moment to make a few important calls in his office. The cool air was a welcome relief as Rob, Tex and Moralez were escorted to their quarters. Josh and Adams were led to the Medical Center to have their wounds checked and their bandages changed. The rest stowed their gear and cleaned up for lunch.

Rob's brother Paul hung up the phone with a smile, glad he'd finished the last of his calls. Everyone was thrilled to hear that Rob was on his way home, and they all asked when he would arrive, but Paul couldn't tell them that. Ashley had promised to pass the word on as soon as she knew herself. Paul had been paying close attention to the reports about the attacks on the terrorists, and all along, he'd been sure Rob was involved in the fight. Now, he was just glad to hear that his brother had survived it all and was on his way home. He mulled over on an idea for a homecoming party, and he decided to call Ashley to get her thoughts about it. "If this isn't a reason to party, I don't know what is!" he told her, and she wholeheartedly agreed.

At the Saudi airbase, Light Force boarded the giant C-140 transport for the final leg of their journey. Meanwhile, the flight crew ran their operation checks as the aircraft was fueled.

In the airbase control tower, one of the flight controllers noticed a blip on the corner of the screen. He tried to identify the radar signature but was unable to do so. Whatever it was, it seemed to be moving too fast. He picked up the comlink and called the Communications Center. The radar technician told him they were already tracking the object. The controller hung up and punched a few keys on the flight computer. Whatever it was, it was heading their way in a hurry, with an ETA of three minutes and closing. Quickly, he summoned Commander Davic on the line and informed him, "Commander, it is highly possible that some type of missile is inbound to our location."

Davic was shaken by the news, but he recovered quickly. He gave the command for battle stations and the base alarms started blaring.

Out on the tarmac, the crew scrambled to pull the fuel line out of the transport.

Rob looked over at Tex and Moralez, his face etched with concern. "The airbase must be under attack! We gotta get the hell outta here right now."

Josh turned to Adams. "Here we go again, buddy. Let's get inside!"

Everyone scrambled for the doors and jumped out of the aircraft. Quickly, they ran for the cover of the red brick and steel building.

Out on the base perimeter, the operators of the Patriot missile defense system punched in the solution to intercept the incoming projectile, then waited anxiously for the green light on the display panel to start blinking. The Scud missile that was heading their way was fired from a mobile launcher the terrorists hijacked from Iraq. As the missile moved within range of the Patriots, the green light blinked as the Patriot system locked on, and the operator released the safety and punched the red button.

The deadly Patriots flashed and streaked out into the sky; it was Scud versus Patriot, in a supersonic race to the death. The Scud made one last adjustment and began to descend toward the target location. The first Patriot missile quickly closed the gap and just missed the incoming Scud. The second Patriot, however, reached maximum velocity as it streaked toward the Scud, then closed in and clipped the Scud tailfins. The impact caused the Patriot to detonate, and the Scud was knocked out of its trajectory. The crippled missile wobbled down into the distant terrain and exploded in a huge, earth-shattering, reddish-orange fireball, so violent that the team felt the building vibrating from the blast.

"Damn!" Josh said, jumping up. "Didn't we just leave all this shit behind us?"

"Calm down, pal, before you rip those stitches," Rob warned. "The Patriots must have taken that Scud out."

The base alarms silenced, and the team cautiously moved back outside to get on their transport. The ground crew and pilots headed for their attack jets. The missile defense system had traced the flight trajectory of the Scud, and they had a lock on the location from which it was fired.

Tex, Rob, and the others watched as the mighty attack jets roared down the runway and punched on their afterburners. The fighters streaked up in a vertical climb, gaining altitude, then disappeared into a vapor trail on the horizon.

Unfortunately for the terrorists, they were too busy celebrating the launch of the Scud to bother getting their mobile launcher on the move. The attack jets closed the gap quickly and locked on to their target. The pilots released their rockets and accelerated into a steep climb. In one fell swoop, the terrorists and Scud launcher were totally obliterated in a firestorm created by several lancer missiles.

About a half-hour west of the Capital, General Smithfield hung up the phone, feeling happy. He had just received word that the final leg of his Light Force team was almost at hand. He sipped his coffee and enjoyed the moment. The noose around his neck had disappeared, and in its place was a huge feather in his hat. The mission was a success, and he was the one who organized it. That would mean another few stars on his uniform.

The phone snapped him out of his daydream. "Yes?" he said.

"You have a staff meeting this morning, General. I just thought I should remind you."

Smithfield thanked his secretary, then hung up. He walked out and handed her the list of the family members of Light Force. "Make the calls and arrange for their transportation to the homecoming," he instructed. He then refilled his coffee, grabbed his briefcase, and headed out for his meeting.

In New Jersey, Paul was just getting ready to leave for work when his phone rang. When he picked up, Agent Foster introduced herself, then informed him that his brother Rob would be arriving in Washington shortly. "The president would like you, Ashley, and your brother Roy to attend the event," she said.

It took a moment for the invitation to sink in, a personal invitation from the president himself. "When?" Paul finally asked when he found his voice again. "And how do we get there?"

"Tomorrow, but don't worry, Paul. Everything is taken care of."

"That's great. I guess I'll let everyone know then."

"Please do and tell them to start packing. There will be a driver at their door by two p.m., to escort them to the airport for the short flight to the Capital. I know you need to make some arrangements, so I will let you go."

Paul hung up the phone and immediately started babbling to himself. "The president? The freaking president? Really?" he said in disbelief as he scrambled around the apartment, looking for his address book. When he found it, Roy was the first one he called. Of course Roy was beside himself with excitement as Paul filled him in on the details of the trip.

Ashley was just about to start her car when her cell phone rang. "Hello?" she said.

"Hey, Ashley, it's Paul. I've got some fantastic news for you."

"Do tell! It's about Rob, right?" she said, with a knot of excitement building in her stomach. "Is he almost home?"

"Yes, and we're all leaving tomorrow afternoon to go see him." When Ashley finally stopped screaming, Paul filled her in on the details.

Again, Rob and the team moved into the C-140, settled into their seats, and buckled up for the long ride home. The aircraft moved across the tarmac and lined up with the runway. The pilot released the brakes and went to full throttle. The huge vessel thundered down the runway and pulled into a steep climb.

When the transport finally leveled off, Tex jumped up. "Next stop, the good ol' U.S. of A.!"

"Amen to that, my man!" Josh added with a smile.

Moralez turned to Rob. "You think we'll get any downtime? I'm beat."

Rob smiled. "I sure hope so. I'm going to request leave for all of us. After the shit we been through, we deserve it."

Tex sat next to Rob. "You got that right. We need a little break."

After lunch, the team gathered around a small table for another game of poker to pass the time. Between hands, everyone jabbered about what he planned to do on leave. Tex wanted to head back to his ranch in Texas and ride his horses. Josh and Adams wanted to spend time with their families, and Moralez couldn't wait to see his sister. As for Rob, he was just looking forward to some peaceful nights with Ashley.

After a few hours, everyone was quiet, and the only sounds were the thrumming of the jet engines. Rob stretched out in his seat for a little sleep, but when he thought about Ashley and her beautiful, smiling face, he felt himself hardening at the thought. He missed her desperately, in every way, and he needed her love now more than ever.

Smithfield moved onto a spacious walkway. In the background, he could see the huge Air Force base as he moved to the doors. He entered the Cy-Com Center and found Agent Foster waiting for him. Together, they needed to go over the agenda one last time, to make sure everything was in order for the arrival of the president and Light Force.

The two walked down a long hallway and entered the newly furnished reception hall. Smithfield felt his feet sinking into the plush carpeting as he looked about the huge space. The event would be attended by invitation only, and the guest list included family members and a select group of military brass, along with cabinet members and a few individuals from the House and Senate. Of course a CNN crew and countless Secret Service agents would be swarming the area.

After every detail was carefully combed over again and again and every possible SNAFU worked out, Smithfield left for some lunch in town.

Chapter 20

Reunion

Ashley hurried back into her condo and called in to work. Her boss wanted to know why she suddenly needed a few days off, but when she told him she'd received a personal invitation from the president, he just laughed in disbelief and hung up the phone. Ashley didn't care if he believed her or not. Her mind was full of thoughts, swirling with pleasant notions of being with Rob and the excitement of meeting the president.

She quickly packed for the trip, making sure to include her nicest outfits, along with the naughty little nighties Rob loved. She could feel her nipples hardening as she tucked the lingerie into the pockets of her suitcase. She was hot and thirsty for his love, now more than ever.

Across the Hudson, Rita sat in her new wheelchair, watching her parents pack. Rita was getting around in the chair fairly well, but she really wanted to be able to walk on her own again, and she wished she could get up and help her parents get ready for their trip to see her brother in Washington. Still, nothing could sour her mood; they were all far too happy and excited ever since they got the good news about Jimmy. Rita was very proud of him and couldn't wait to see his smiling face, even if she had to look up at it from a wheelchair.

The C-140 transport made good speed, with the help of a tailwind. The pilot checked the onboard computer display and saw that they were about to enter U.S. airspace over the Gulf of Mexico. The comlink lit up, indicating an incoming call; the flight control tower at Eglin Air Force base in Florida had picked them up on their radar. They went through the usual security and flight checks and heading coordinates, and all was well.

The cabin lights flickered on, and the pilot announced they were about to enter U.S. airspace, just three hours from touchdown.

Tex was the first to snap awake. He looked around and, to his delight, saw that everyone else was fast asleep. When he spotted Rob, he came up with a devious revenge plan.

Slowly, Tex moved to the tray table and grabbed the pitcher full of ice water. Ever so slowly, he moved toward Rob, who was sleeping with his blanket pulled partly up over his head. Josh had stirred and was now awake in the seat behind Rob, struggling to hold in his chuckle as he watched Tex slowly pull Rob's blanket down, then move behind him and unload the entire pitcher of ice water over his head.

Rob jerked awake. "What the…?" he shouted, his face twisted with rage. "What the frig?" he yelled, jumping to his feet and looking around as water dripped from his hair and off the tip of his nose. "You!" he said, pointing at Tex as everyone in the surrounding chairs woke up and immediately started laughing.

Tex tried to compose himself as he replied, "Like I've told you a million times, payback's a bitch!"

Rob's stern face broke into a smile. "You got me, you sucker! From now on, it's every man for himself."

Tex handed him a towel. "You'll get over it, my friend. I did."

They looked up and saw the co-pilot standing in the cabin doorway, looking none too pleased as he glanced around at the messy cabin and the wet floor. "What's all the ruckus about?" he asked, crossing his arm and scrunching up his face.

"Sorry. We were just—" Rob started, but the co-pilot held a hand up to stop him.

"I thought they said all you boys were housebroken," he said, looking at Rob's soaked clothes. His stern expression then melted into a grin. "Looks like you guys are having a little fun."

Tex pointed at Rob. "It's all his fault. He started it."

The silence lasted a moment before the cabin echoed with laughter again.

Before the chuckling co-pilot left, he informed them they were making good speed toward touchdown.

Josh brought out the cards, and everyone settled in for a nap or another game of poker to pass the time.

Paul, Roy, and Ashley could hardly contain their excitement as they rode the airliner, heading south, to the airbase. They'd been talking for over an hour about New York City, Rob, and what it was going to be like to meet the president in person. Now, all was quiet, except for the gentle, endless humming of the jet engines. Ashley was deep in thought, longing for her friend and lover. Gradually, her eyes closed, and she drifted into Dreamland.

After another hour of quiet, the flight assistant turned on the cabin lights, and the pilot's voice came over the intercom, "We are beginning our descent and should be on the ground and at our gate just about on time."

Everyone stirred in their seats as the flight assistant walked down the aisle, giving them instructions for a safe landing: "Seat backs up and safety belts on please."

Ashley took a long swig from her Coke, hoping it would wake her up. She felt the plane descending as she took out a hand towel and wiped the sleep from her eyes.

"You were really out of it," Paul said, looking at her from his seat across the aisle. "For some reason, I just can't sleep on a plane."

Just as he finished talking, the aircraft dropped into a wide turn, and the landing gear engaged with a loud thud.

"Here we go!" Roy yelled, with all the excitement of a kid on a rollercoaster. In another life, Roy might have chosen to be a pilot himself. Planes had always fascinated him, and he could think of nothing cooler than being in control of the throttle of such a massive machine.

The pilot guided the aircraft to fall in line with the runway. The plane came in heads up, floated over the runway, and gently touched down.

Ashley was suddenly wide awake, smacked with the realization that she would see Rob very soon. She couldn't wait to be in his arms again.

On the outskirts of the Capital, the Air Force base was a buzz of activity as they prepared for the arrival of Light Force. CNN trucks were already arriving; select journalists had been briefed by the Secret Service on the security procedures concerning the president's arrival and the privacy concerns when it came to filming the Special Forces team. They were authorized to film them, but they had to block or blur their faces, or the film would be confiscated and destroyed.

The aircraft taxied to the gate and shut down. The doors opened, and Paul, Roy, and Ashley were greeted in the terminal by General Smithfield's assistants. The group exited the back door of the terminal and was quickly escorted into a large white van for the ride across the airfield, to the Cy-Com Center. Roy was in awe as he watched a fighter jet moving on the concourse.

Ashley turned to Paul. "Just look at the size of this place. I'm excited about Rob, but I'm nervous about meeting the president."

Paul smiled. "This whole situation is a little overwhelming, but I think we'll all be fine."

Roy also smiled. "I think it's awesome. I'm so proud of Rob. If you're so nervous about meeting the president, just do what I did when I was nervous about my driving instructor and flunking the test after high school."

"And what's that?" Ashley asked.

"Imagine him in his underwear!"

Ashley's face brightened with the blush of embarrassment. "I'd rather imagine your brother that way," she said. "I can't wait to see him!"

The van pulled up to the front entrance, and the group moved inside the massive red brick, glass, and gray steel building that was Cy-Com.

General Smithfield stepped forward and introduced himself. "Welcome, everyone! We have been expecting you."

As Ashley introduced herself to the general, she couldn't help but notice all the stars on his uniform.

"It won't be long before the troops arrive," the general said. "We have accommodations set up for everyone. You will have some time to welcome them back before the president arrives. My assistant will show you the way."

Ashley felt her excitement swelling as they were escorted down a long hallway. Paul and Roy were impressed as they entered a large, nicely furnished room that reminded Paul of one of the lounges at the airport. Ashley noticed a woman in a wheelchair, so after she helped herself to some coffee, she walked over to talk to her. Paul and Roy took the seats facing a large window and watched the action out on the airfield.

In the transport, Light Force was immersed in deep conversation.

"You can keep your steak and apple pie," Rob said to Tex. "I'm going straight to that little restaurant by our condo, and I'm gonna order barbecue ribs and a couple ice-cold mugs of stout on tap. Those ribs are so juicy and tender they almost fall off the bone. Then, my friends, we're gonna pick up a bottle of Jack and head directly to our bedroom."

Tex smiled. "Listen, when I say steak, I'm talkin' Texas T-bone. It's like no other, my friend."

Moralez stood up. "Enough already! I'm getting damn hungry."

Just as he finished talking, the co-pilot entered the cabin, "We are starting our descent. We should be on the ground in about a half-hour."

Butterflies danced in Rob's stomach. He'd been on many missions, but this one really had him worried he would never see home again.

The transport banked into a wide, sweeping turn before it took a quick downward plunge. The giant aircraft was nose up as the pilot lined up with the runway, and everyone in the cabin felt the landing gear drop.

"Honeys, we're home!" Tex yelled.

The transport touched down on the runway, and Rob and his buddies immediately hooted and hollered, celebrating the end of a very long, very difficult journey.

Roy jumped out of his chair, "Look!" he said, pointing out to a large military aircraft as it taxied off the runway.

Paul ran to the window. "I bet that's our guys!"

Everyone crowded around him and watched the huge plane as it slowly turned and moved out of view.

One of the general's assistants entered the room and smiled at the gathering around the glass. "Yes, that's our plane," he said. "Your loved ones have arrived."

"Oh my God! I can't wait to see Rob." Ashley said, hurrying toward the door. "C'mon! Let's go, guys!"

The assistant stood by the door, holding up his hand. "I realize how anxious you must be to see them, but please hold on for a little while longer. The general will bring them here after their debriefing. It shouldn't take very long."

"Try to relax," Paul said, gently taking Ashley by the elbow when he saw the disappointment in her face. "The important thing is that Rob and his comrades are home."

The transport doors opened, and everyone gathered their gear and exited the aircraft, into the bright sunshine of a beautiful late summer day. On the tarmac, Rob dropped down on his knees and placed his hand on the ground. Slowly, he made the sign of the cross on his chest and thanked God for his safe return, then actually leaned over and kissed the asphalt.

Tex yelled, "Sure good to be back!"

The general's assistants welcomed them first, then escorted them all to their temporary quarters. Before they left, one of the escorts informed them that he would be back in a little while. "The general is most eager to see you," he said. "Please change, if you will."

Rob looked over at their spotless dress uniforms, crisp and freshly ironed, neatly arranged on the wall. "Time to put on our Sunday best, fellas," he said. "We've got big-wigs to impress."

The team finished dressing and helped themselves to fresh coffee and sandwiches from a nearby table. In a matter of minutes, their escort arrived, and Rob and the team were led to the meeting room.

Agent Foster and General Smithfield walked out the front entrance of Cy-Com to take a quick ride across the airfield to the debriefing.

Full of excitement, General Smithfield jumped out of his seat and approached his team with a smile. "Welcome home, boys! You had us worried, praying for this day."

Rob stepped forward. "Thank you, sir. It's good to be back."

As soon as everyone was seated, Smithfield got underway with the very brief debriefing. "I want to take this moment to commend each and every one of you for eliminating the threat. My job was on the line, many lives were on the line, and you men pulled through. I will never, ever forget that."

After a general outline of what happened during the mission, the debriefing was adjourned, and another round of handshakes was shared, along with many thanks and congratulations for a job well done.

Inside Cy-Com, CNN crews were set up and waiting for the president's arrival. A large assortment of political and military personnel arrived and was immediately escorted into the spacious meeting hall.

The general told Rob and the others that they would have about thirty minutes of personal time to spend with their families, and when they finally got there, Rob was the first one through the door. He immediately spotted Ashley, beaming that unforgettable smile at him from across the room.

"Rob!" Ashley screamed. "Oh my God!" She scrambled across the room and jumped into his arms, and they embraced and shared a long kiss.

All around the room tears of joy began to flow. Rita was so excited to see Jimmy that she stood from her wheelchair and mastered a step on her own. Moralez was overcome with emotion as he hugged his dear sister.

Paul stepped forward and gave his brother a hug. "Welcome back. We're happy to see you."

Roy added, "My brother, the hero! Man, it's good to have you home, Rob."

"Oh, I don't know about that hero thing," Rob retorted. "I'm just glad to see my brothers and my woman again," he said, keeping his arm tightly around Ashley's waist.

A few minutes later, Ashley pulled Rob away from his brothers, and they sat down. He looked into her eyes. "The general said we'll have more time after the meeting," he said.

She pulled out a set of keys and wiggled them in front of him, looking at him with a playful twinkle in her eyes. "Good, because I booked us a room at the Hilton."

Rob smiled and felt himself hardening again as his lips touched hers. He whispered in her ear, "To hell with the president. Let's go right now."

The two of them stared at each other for a moment before the laughter took over; their hunger would have to wait a little bit longer.

The room soon quieted, and after family time was over, Rob and the team were led to the meeting hall. As they entered and made their way to the stage, they received a standing ovation. Rob actually blushed when he looked out at the sea of people, especially the military brass, giving him accolades and applauding.

One of the general's aids instructed Light Force to line up in formation, and the CNN cameras zoomed in on the stage. The president was backstage, waiting with his Secret Service escort. General Smithfield stood at the front of the formation, basking in his own portion of the fame and glory.

Secretary of Defense Moreland moved to the podium, and the crowd quieted down. Moreland looked around the crowded room. "I want to thank all of you for coming on such short notice. It is my pleasure to introduce the president of the United States!"

The room broke out in another round of applause as the commander-in-chief took center stage.

He turned with a smile and pointed at Light Force, and everyone jumped to their feet and began to cheer again.

Rob felt the hairs on the back of his neck stand up, and he was overcome with emotion as the president smiled at him and bowed a bit, showing his approval.

Starting with General Smithfield, the president shook hands with everyone onstage. When he reached the podium, the entire room grew dead quiet, awaiting his speech.

Caught up in the moment, Ashley was on the verge of tears. She was very proud of Rob, who was smiling at her as he stood at attention onstage. The medals on his uniform sparked in the lights from the cameras, and Ashley's eyes sparkled with pride.

"On behalf of the American people, I want to express, to all involved in this critical mission, our heartfelt gratitude for eliminating the deadly threat." The president then knowingly turned to the camera. "I want to assure each and every one of you, my fellow citizens that we will not stop until justice has been served!"

The president paused, waiting for another round of applause to simmer down, then turned to his troops. "While our hearts do break for the needless loss of innocent life in Iraq due to these terrorist acts, I want to thank you for saving untold American lives. For actions above and beyond the call of duty, it is my pleasure to present to all of you, the Congressional Medal of Honor."

Again, there was a standing ovation, and the filming of the gathering hit the networks and spread across the land almost instantaneously. After the horror of 9/11, it was a good thing to have something to cheer about.

There seemed to be electric in the air as the president slowly moved down the line of soldiers, presenting each of them with a medal of high esteem for their valiant efforts.

Rob stood at attention as the president moved to him and shook his hand with a smile.

"I'm very proud of you, Lt. Marrino. In honor of your bravery in action," the president said, then placed a blue ribbon with a shiny medal around Rob's neck.

"Thank you, sir," Rob replied, his voice uncharacteristically shaky as he saluted the president.

The president smiled and moved out into the crowd to greet some friends. The meeting was adjourned by Moreland. General Smithfield and the president shook hands with some of the military brass, and Rob and the team were escorted back to their quarters to collect their personal belongings. They were granted a month's leave, effective immediately, so everyone had someone to call or someplace to go for the night. The next morning, Light Force would be at Arlington National Cemetery, where Phil Takis would be buried with full military honors.

Rob and the others departed the base. Rob followed Ashley to her car, and they drove through the heavy traffic, toward the Hilton. They decided to have dinner at the hotel restaurant.

Rob was deep in thought as they pulled in front of the hotel. There was something important he had to talk to Ashley about, something that couldn't wait even a day longer. The ring would come as soon as they could find some free time for shopping, something special and just for her, but he simply couldn't put off popping the question.

They unloaded their bags from the car, and the doorman called for a bellhop to take their things to their room. They stepped into the plush lobby and checked in, then headed to the restaurant for dinner.

Rob asked for a corner booth by the fireplace, then ordered a bottle of their finest champagne, as well as two gourmet dinners for them both. It didn't take long for the delicious, steaming-hot food to arrive, and they enjoyed their entrées and the crisp, cold bubbly.

After dinner, Rob led Ashley to the dance floor. He pulled her close, and they slow-danced to the mellow music, enjoying the closeness they had both missed so much.

By the time the song finished, Rob knew the moment had come. He held her hand in his and dropped to one knee. "Ashley, baby, will you marry me?" he asked, looking up into her eyes.

Ashley's eyes brightened, and her face blushed. "Yes! Yes, I will, Rob. I'll marry you!" she shrieked, then jumped up and down in excitement.

Rob felt his heart pounding in his chest. He stood and pulled her into a long, deep kiss.

Everyone on the dance floor turned their attention on the couple and clapped, looking adoringly—and some quite enviously—at the handsome soldier with the beautiful lady.

Later that night, Rob and Ashley were in bed, panting after hours of passionate lovemaking that had started on the couch and ended up in the king-sized bed at the Hilton.

"I've got something for you," Ashley whispered.

Rob smiled. "I'm home, and I have you, and I have my family. What else could I possibly want right now?"

Ashley's eyes widened. "I promise you'll really like it."

"Okay, okay. Let's see it then."

Ashley jumped out of bed and returned with a tray full of goodies, including a half-gallon of Rob's favorite rocky road ice cream.

"Oh my God!" Rob said as Ashley handed him the tray and jumped back in bed. "I love you so much, baby, but where's the whipped cream?"

Ashley's face tightened, and she was quiet for a moment before she joined him in a silly laugh.

In the early hours of the morning, the tray lay empty on the floor. With their energy spent, both of them were wrapped together, but deep inside Ashley, something was happening during her sound slumber. Ever so slowly, the miracle of new life was beginning. Their lives would never be quite the same again. For them, things would be even better.

The following morning broke crisp and clear. Rob and the rest of Light Force arrived at Arlington National Cemetery and were escorted to the gravesite of Phil Takis.

Rob noticed Phil's wife Emily sitting near the burial site, and he knelt down before her, "I am so sorry for your loss." He fought back the tears welling in his eyes. "Phil was a good man, a brave soldier."

Emily stood, and they embraced each other. "Thank you," she replied, "and yes, yes he was."

Rob struggled to gather his composure as he moved back in formation and tried to settle down.

General Smithfield arrived with Agent Foster and the secretary Mooreland. Light Force stood at attention as the Honor Guard arrived with the flag-covered coffin of their comrade. Rob watched as the white-gloved soldiers moved with slow precision and placed the coffin at the gravesite.

The somber ceremony lasted another half-hour, and Phil was laid to rest with full military honors.

Afterward, Rob, his brothers, and Ashley climbed into their limousine for the ride to the airport. For Rob, at that moment, with the ones he loved, nothing else mattered. *Damn, it's just so good to be home,* he thought, giving his fiancée's hand a squeeze as the scenery blurred by outside.

In September of 2014, Rob, Ashley, and their 12-year-old son, Steven, were just getting off the ferry. They walked along the dock on the shores of Manhattan. It was a beautiful, late summer day, with just a few puffy, white clouds drifting in the bright blue sky. Rob was eager to see the new memorial at ground zero. They moved along the crowded sidewalks.

"Dad, look at all the trees!" Steven yelled as they were just about to enter the outskirts of the memorial plaza.

"Oh my God! It's beautiful," Ashley said, as her mind flashed back to the destruction of 9/11.

As they moved through the plaza, filled with white oaks, Rob stopped for a moment to take in the earthy smell, and a feeling of renewal and peace overcame him. The family was gradually drawn to the edge of memorial. Rob stared into the gigantic void that was once the base of the first tower. The water was gently moving down the sides, into the darkness. His mind flashed back to that horrible day of shock and horror. He knelt down and prayed for the victims and their families.

Steven was silent, overcome with the enormity of it all, but he followed his mother as she walked the edge of the void, looking at all the names engraved in the golden metal. She stared at the gently flowing water and felt a sense of permanence, of spirituality, and of peace there, at that absolutely beautiful memorial.

"I'm thirsty," Rob said to Ashley. "Let's sit under the trees and take a break."

Steven smiled and hugged his mother. "Good. I'm hungry, Mom."

They found a bench, and Ashley opened her day bag. Dark chocolate protein bars, water, and fresh apples were on the menu.

Rob sat back, sighed, and took a long swallow from his bottle of water. Suddenly, Steven pointed and yelled, "Look, Daddy!"

Rob glanced up at Freedom Tower and was overwhelmed by its magnificence, a towering tribute to the people of New York. The glass and steel exterior brightly glowed in a golden halo of sunlight. In that moment, his mind flashed back to his fight in Iraq, and his Brother Paul's words: *"Freedoms' light! May it burn forever!"*

Made in the USA
Charleston, SC
15 January 2017